Terrified and feeling like an uninvited guest at the all-boys St. Stephen's School, Mauricio Londoño sets his main goal for freshman year: basic survival. But despite his efforts to tiptoe through the school year, Mauricio can't resist the allure of the world inhabited by his precocious classmates and the drama that plays out on FaceSpace. When a cruel digital scheme sweeps through the school, Mauricio not only becomes one of its victims but also starts to think that maybe it's not so bad to be honest about who he really is.

initiation

SUSAN FINE

initiation

Woodbury, Minnesota

First Edition
Second Printing, 2010

Book design by Steffani Sawyer
Cover design by Kevin R. Brown

Flux, an imprint of Llewellyn Publications

Library of Congress Cataloging-in-Publication Data
Fine, Susan.
  Initiation / Susan Fine.—1st ed.
     p. cm.
  Summary: A prestigious New York City prep school for boys becomes embroiled in scandal during Mauricio's freshman year.
  ISBN 978-0-7387-1466-0
  [1. Preparatory schools—Fiction. 2. High schools—Fiction. 3. Schools—Fiction. 4. New York (N.Y.)—Fiction.] I. Title.
  PZ7.F495679In 2009
  [Fic]—dc22
                                    2008053352

Flux
Llewellyn Publications
A Division of Llewellyn Worldwide, Ltd.
2143 Wooddale Drive, Dept. 978-0-7387-1466-0
Woodbury, MN 55125-2989, U.S.A.
www.fluxnow.com

Printed in the United States of America

Acknowledgments

Several loyal supporters made *Initiation* possible. My agent, Laura Dail, brought the perfect blend of optimism and pragmatism to the project, and I am very grateful for her encouragement and support. My fantastic friend and former colleague Laura Dickerman is an extraordinary editor, and *Initiation* would have never made it to publication without her wisdom and the meticulous comments she made on several versions of the manuscript.

Andrew Karre, my first editor at Flux, was enthusiastic about the novel early on and had wonderful insights about how to make the book better. Brian Farrey, my second editor at Flux, has shared Andrew's enthusiasm, despite inheriting me and my novel with little say in the matter. I am happy and relieved that this inheritance has not been akin to receiving a beat-up old car or an out-of-tune piano from an aged relative. Other members of the Flux team, especially Sandy Sullivan, Marissa Pederson, and Courtney Huber, deserve many, many thanks for their hard work on *Initiation*.

Finally, my husband, Matt Horvat, patiently listened to me read aloud every word I wrote in every draft of *Initiation*, over what has to be more than a year. That's a lot of patient listening. Then, of course, he offered numerous helpful suggestions, some along the lines of, "No ninth grade boy would ever say that." His experiences as a boy, as a boy who went to a boys' school, and as a person who has worked with several thousand adolescent boys were invaluable for my novel.

It isn't given to us to know those rare moments when people are wide open and the lightest touch can wither or heal. A moment too late and we can never reach them any more in this world.

—F. Scott Fitzgerald, "The Freshest Boy"

1

The minute I walked into the St. Stephen's School for Boys, I began to sweat. There was still no air conditioning, and the temperature inside was higher than it was outside. I used to think that maybe one day I would be a rich man; then I would send a pile of money to the school, earmarked for air conditioning. I would be the big shot who cooled the place off. Mauricio Londoño: Air Conditioning King... King Cool... Mr. Freeze... Prince Frosty... LL Cool... something.

I used to dream about that kind of thing all the time. And I still wanted to be rich—ridiculously rich, but I wasn't so sure anymore about giving a bunch of cash to St. Stephen's. Despite how hot I was, maybe everyone here needed to sweat it out. Endure the misery as I had, and as every guy before me had. The St. Stephen's rite of sweltering passage.

But right when I walked into the building that day, I knew. I knew that no matter what I endured or accomplished, how much I sweated it out, how much money I earned, or even if the *New York Times* or the *Wall Street Journal* applauded some phenomenal accomplishment of mine, I would always be the pathetic ninth grader I had been on my first day at that place.

It was as if my eighteen-year-old body was an empty shell housing that punk high school freshman. I would never stop being the scrawny boy who walked the halls, scared, anxious, and stooped under the weight of an enormous backpack. And worst of all, I was still waiting for a goddamn golden ticket—access to something—even now. Yet I had managed to survive ninth grade, and all the rest of it, when five of my classmates hadn't. There were a bunch of casualties from that whole mess freshman year.

No matter what was going on in that place, it was always hot inside, an inferno. The heat *and* the noise were oppressive. A lot of people thought that St. Stephen's was the hottest school in the city, but they didn't get that the adjective was about the temperature, not the billions of guys who went on to Ivy League colleges or anything like that. St. Stephen's School for Boys was the hottest, loudest private school in Manhattan. Maybe that's what comes from stuffing eight hundred blue-blazered boys into one building, where fifteen floors filled with classrooms and libraries and lunchrooms and science labs stacked and buried desperate kids right on top of each other.

Even the kindergartners in that place were desperate. They all wanted to be the top dog with the most Pokémon cards. By ninth grade the stakes changed—the terms of our attempts to prove ourselves and one-up each other were different, but underneath all that, it was the same old story, the timeless male legend, the eternal saga of proving who has the biggest dick. My classmates and I spent most of our energy trying to sort that out. Mostly we discovered who *was* the biggest dick.

But what always lurked beneath our endless squabbles and daily drills was that desperation. I had no idea, when I started there, how much the school tie would come to feel like a noose. Yet somehow my faith in St. Stephen's, my desire to belong, never evaporated—not even after my first year, when everything and then some unraveled.

I had graduated from St. Stephen's about a month ago. Before graduation, I thought all the time about how it was almost over, how I didn't ever have to go back into that loud inferno again, how I was finished with that place and would head off to college and be done. I kept trying to figure out whether it had all been worth it. All that happened my first year—it kind of lingered, way in the back of my mind, sort of buzzing around back there like a trapped fly.

Then I won a big fancy award at graduation, and I got sucked back in. Like the keys to the castle were right there, jingling in front of my face, beckoning me back and promising me something incredible.

What I wanted now, why I'd come back to the school a couple weeks after graduation, was to find my name. It had been carved into one of the five million plaques lining the walls of the main foyer announcing all the names of students who had distinguished themselves at the St. Stephen's School for Boys. I had to see the evidence to be sure that the award wasn't just another fantasy.

It was the Headmaster's Award—the "nice guy" award—the one they give to the good kid who isn't the best student or athlete or thespian or fencer or soccer player or mathematician or cellist or poker player or anything else, but even so deserves to win *something*—deserves to have some bone thrown to him. I was the decent guy who did his homework. The guy who didn't cheat. The guy who was on time. The guy who was in dress code. The guy who didn't think he knew more than the teachers; or if he did, he shut his fat trap and didn't let anyone else know. The guy who *mostly* didn't smoke or drink or hook up and, no matter what, kept showing up on time every day. The boring guy who nobody wanted to throttle but nobody cared about either. The guy who tried like hell to be good at something—anything. The guy who *wasn't* the biggest dick.

At least that's what people believed about me. And, for as long as St. Stephen's continued to exist, eight hundred boys would walk down that hall and believe it, too.

I had done more than survive. The plaque confirmed my triumph. I wanted to see it. I *needed* to see it.

Although I wasn't so eager anymore to get out of there and never come back, it felt as if the whole thing had caught me, kind of like a fish on a hook, and reeled me back in. But the hook was stuck in my mouth now, and it wasn't clear whether this was catch-and-release or what. Maybe I'd spend the rest of my life with a hook stuck in my face.

I didn't rush over to the plaque. I was measured and cool, or as cool as I could be with sweat running down the sides of my face and dampening my hair. I could feel my shirt sticking to my back, but I had learned at St. Stephen's how to appear calm and confident, sure and certain of myself, cool and composed, no matter how I felt. Never reveal anything. That was a huge St. Stephen's lesson: the deadpan. Even in the face of total disaster, show no sign of trouble, not even the twitch of an eyebrow. My ex-friend Henry Steel was the master of this. Hide it all or risk having everybody know your secret shit, your vulnerabilities, your weaknesses. Hide it all even if the efforts to do so gnaw through your body like a cancerous tumor.

But even at the moment when I was about to see myself immortalized—forever a part of St. Stephen's history and glory and its ten million traditions and honors and all that—and even though I had become somewhat skilled at the St. Stephen's deadpan, it felt as though something inside of me was rotting. Something was decaying and threatening to poison me or—even worse—leak out, right along with my confession that I really wasn't sure about anything.

I had never felt this way before I went to St. Stephen's, and I never stopped feeling this way after that first year. But I kept getting up every morning and getting dressed and showing up on time. Hell, I was still desperate to be the St. Stephen's "gentleman" everyone promised I would become, regardless of how much deception and decay lurked beneath the shiny marble façade of that school and within my own heart.

Then I saw it. Hanging in the middle of the wall, right in the main foyer of the fabulous, famous St. Stephen's School for Boys, was my name on the plaque. But it wasn't *my* name. It was Mauricio Londoño's.

What a goddamn surprise. They had always gotten it wrong. I was Mauricio Londono at St. Stephen's. It was too much trouble to figure out how to make the "ñ" on the computer. Despite all the foreign languages taught, everything from Mandarin to German, French, Spanish, and Italian (along with a couple of dead languages), somehow the registrar couldn't make the "ñ."

He needed the boss I had last summer at a crappy copyediting internship. That guy was always screaming about the difference between the em dash and the en dash, like it was some kind of life-or-death matter. No one was screaming at the registrar at St. Stephen's; no one was holding a gun to his head, telling him to figure out the "ñ" or hit the road. Hell, no one was even politely asking him to learn how to use *Word*.

Now here I was, almost four years after my first day of ninth grade, the year that changed everything, the year when it all began. Yet I was still fourteen-year-old Mauricio Londoño, sitting on one of the old wooden benches in the main foyer, waiting and hoping for my life to make sense—somehow still believing that the school mattered and that it could make me matter.

fall

2

I walked into the upper school assembly, and it was as though I had stepped on a beehive. All around me boys of every shape and size swarmed. Guys were running around, pounding each other on the back, and whooping it up. They yelled and backslapped and punched each other in the arm with abandon. I looked out across the room, wondering where I had landed, and what stood out as much as all that intense activity was how the whole room was like a huge sea of blue blazers.

There wasn't one barrette or hair ribbon anywhere. No pastel-colored sweaters or pink T-shirts, backpacks with a thousand Hello Kitty key chains hanging off them, pencil bags with smiley faces on them and pens in every color inside, or strappy sandals, lip gloss, or anything. The squeals that had driven me nuts in eighth grade, shocking and thrilling me when they burst out of small clusters of whispering girls, were gone. It felt like losing an annoying cousin, whose presence at Thanksgiving was part of the annual routine.

But now as I stood in the back of that room, I was lost in that big blue sea, floating aimlessly in that turbulent ocean on some homemade raft, and all around me were these big honking yachts, full of sailors whose sea legs had developed over a gazillion years of sailing and boating in the tropics. This school was theirs, and as I watched them jumping into their seats and slouching down, leaning over each other to talk to guys down the row or just give a high five or something, it was clear that they were as comfortable here as they were in their own living rooms.

Right when I was trying to decide whether to risk entering the frenzied hive or run like hell out of there, an older man came up to me.

"Freshman?" I nodded. "Up front, on the right," he said, pointing toward the front of the room.

"Thanks," I mumbled, then took a deep breath and started creeping slowly toward an empty aisle seat I'd spotted near the front. Right then a trio of seniors barged by, pushing me into a row of seats as they made their way down the middle aisle. When I finally managed to fold myself into the seat, hoping like anything to blend into the blue sea, one senior who was high-fiving all his friends, backslapping and hugging all over the place, did this big dive right over me and several other guys to grab some kid a couple seats down. I tried to see what he was doing, but with his body crushing my head, I could barely make out that he was rumpling the kid's hair. I heard him shout, "Hey, baby! How ya doin'?" I was relieved when he moved along, although he rapped each freshman between "baby" and the aisle on the head as he wiggled himself up and off us.

While freshmen sat in the front-right section, across from the seniors, we could just as well have been organized according to facial hair (or lack thereof). Most of the freshmen had little more than peach fuzz above their upper lips, while many of the seniors were freshly shaved—or, what was more common, in need of a shave, with a few of them sporting carefully crafted goatees or scraggly mustaches accompanied by long sideburns.

There were adults scurrying around, trying to settle the boys down but also joining in on all the backslapping along with a whole bunch of handshaking. I had never before, at any school, seen this many joking and back-and-forth exchanges between adults and kids. For God's sake, these were teachers.

When the head of the upper school walked onto the stage and spoke into the microphone at the podium, the noise wound down, as though someone were turning the volume knob slowly to the left, easing us into a short break from the tumult. Row after row of boys filled the theater, and we sat there in silence, lined up, waiting for school to begin.

By now I had taken a couple of deep breaths and sort of settled into my seat, but I was feeling this intense mix of anxiety, excitement, and awe. I had never been part of anything like this in my life, but I had fallen in love with the school during my admissions visit. Everything in the school looked new and expensive, from the dark red velvet curtains hanging down behind the podium on the stage to the trays in the lunchroom, which had the school's insignia right in the center of them. For some reason, the lunchroom trays had stuck in my mind ever since that first visit. I wanted to go to school in that setting, I wanted to become the fine young gentleman that the school's mission statement promised to make me, and I wanted to eat my lunch off a tray that proclaimed the school's motto in Latin: *Mens sana in corpore sano*. Mostly, though, I wanted to be important. That seemed to be the promise of the place.

Now, early in the morning on that first day of school, I sat in the assembly hall like a frightened mouse. Staring at the dark red curtains and thinking about those trays, I wondered what would happen next.

In that moment, as we all sat there waiting, it was as though we were taking collective breaths—like we were inhaling and exhaling together. There was a strange tension percolating, as if at any second some surprising or shocking event would take place. The energy in the room was palpable. We were all waiting for something to happen, and it wasn't clear whether it would be wonderful or horrible.

On that first day of ninth grade, I had no idea what could come of packing all those boys into one school building. I could not have imagined how the competition would play out—in relentless insults and the constant sorting that went on all day, every day, to determine who was okay and who was worthless. Of course, there were several kinds of worthless: some boys were worthless and basically nonexistent; others were worthless and should get their asses kicked.

The No Fighting rule meant these boys had to be verbally attacked for everything from the shoes they wore to their mothers' names, their families' cars, the stupid little dogs they had, the way they laughed or sneezed or hiccupped or farted or chewed their food or anything that others could detect and seize on, leap on and rip to shreds. And everyone's position was always changing. Very little was secure; we were all trying to swim in quicksand, and it was a daily drill to spot weaknesses and attack them as if we were fighting a war. Everything was always right there on the edge, threatening to go over it so that we destroyed each other. But then at the last moment—just as I witnessed on that first day in the assembly hall—something or someone would rein in all that incredible noise.

3

From the stage, Mr. Michael Mitzenmacher looked out at us and nodded. "Gentlemen, welcome back. Welcome to the 274th year of this grand old school." Before his final word was out, the seniors began to cheer. Almost immediately every boy in the room was shouting at the top of his lungs, and then everyone began to stomp his feet. The sound was deafening, but also addictive. There was something alluring about joining in with the noise-making, and it made me feel less anxious to throw my voice into the cacophony and stomp my feet. My body began to relax as my shouts and stomps joined those of the two hundred and ninety-nine boys who surrounded me. I could have been at a hockey game, I thought as I pounded my feet into the concrete floor as hard as I could. Finally, there was something to do, and I was eager to do anything that would take the edge off the feeling that was threatening to make me throw up all over the floor.

But just as quickly as the noise started, it ended. What had seemed eternal was over in a minute. There was the head of the upper school, smiling down on us from the stage, relieved the noise was over but energized by it himself.

His face was flushed, and he spoke with an excited eagerness. "Gentlemen, now I *know* that I am back at the St. Stephen's School for Boys. While the summer is an important time for taking care of the school, readying it for the forthcoming year, the lifeblood of the school—our beloved students, our *raison d'être*—is gone." His voice shifted with the French phrase, and with four syllables he established the quality of his foreign studies. My mother, who was French, would have been impressed. "Welcome back," he continued. "I wish you the best for the school year."

Mr. Mitzenmacher was a large man, well over six feet tall. He leaned over a little when he was speaking into the microphone. I thought about how he'd shaken my hand firmly when I entered the assembly hall, looking right at me and addressing me by name. He knew all the students' names and even went beyond names to the hobbies we had listed in our applications. He let us know he had read our files without saying so. The returning boys addressed him as Mr. Mitz, but I soon learned they all called him Mitzy.

"Gentlemen, we all know that the faculty at St. Stephen's is like no other in the country, perhaps even the world. We have the most talented teachers anywhere, and, of course, we need such skill and talent—such masters and scholars—because we have the best and brightest students. Today I'd like to introduce two new faculty members— but first, let us thank all of your teachers for everything these masters and scholars do in their service to this noble institution." The room again exploded with clapping and cheering, followed by more stomping. Mr. Mitz held his hands up high, and after a couple of long minutes, the noise subsided. "Both of our new teachers bring excellent experience and impressive credentials to St. Stephen's."

The first new teacher, Mr. Nathan Hawthorne, had been an "oarsman" during his years at Yale—whatever an oarsman was. He had started a boating company somewhere in Massachusetts when he was in high school. His face looked like brown shoe leather. He was an expert in ancient cultures and was going to teach world history to freshmen and an archeology elective to juniors and seniors. He didn't seem to mind all of us scrutinizing him and smiled as he rocked back and forth.

It was with the second introduction that the atmosphere in the room changed. The humidity had been thick when we walked in, but it now became instantly heavier.

At any moment, sweat threatened to drip from the ceiling and run down the walls.

I had seen a few female teachers in the auditorium before the assembly started, but they were all stout and gray and more like a librarian or an elderly aunt than anybody this crowd would have stopped to look at. None of them were capable of making the thick, heavy atmosphere even more so or quickening the pace of every boy's heart.

The second new teacher was young and beautiful, and the collective organism that was that roomful of three hundred high school boys was in agreement about this. The small whispers and muffled laughs that accompanied Mr. Mitz's first introduction disappeared, and the room now assumed an unusual quietness, as if everyone in there was holding his breath and trying not to let anybody notice how excited he was.

She stood at the back of the auditorium and briefly held up her hand when Mr. Mitz began his description of her life and work before St. Stephen's. I couldn't stop looking at her and wondering what she was doing in this room—this sweaty, smelly, noisy room. Mr. Mitz said something about a PhD and intellectual something or another, but to this day I cannot remember anything other than what she looked like. That image was burned into my brain and still thrills me when I pull it up and bring it into focus.

She had smooth light skin, which contrasted with her long dark hair and blue eyes. Her eyes were super blue, noticeably so, deep, deep blue, and across her nose was a sprinkling of freckles. She was beautiful and cute at the same time, and she couldn't have been more different from the gray ladies, who were like normal teachers. She was wearing a pale yellow sweater that looked so soft that I started thinking about touching it. I wondered what she would do if I did. She was small and curvy, and the sweater clung to her chest. I couldn't stop thinking about her tits. I imagined they had to be as soft as her sweater.

I stared at her and squeezed my hands together in my lap. My hands now felt like enormous clumsy clubs, and I looked at her hands, one of which was resting on the side of her face. She had fingernails that were shaped like little moons, little red moons. Even from where I was sitting across the room, I could see the bright red polish on her nails. I wondered what she was thinking about as she gazed out at the rows of boys, who were all staring at her and thinking the same hungry thought.

Apparently she was going to teach French and Spanish. I thought about how I would be able to talk to her in both languages, and I was trying to decide whether I should address her as Señorita or Mademoiselle when I heard Mr. Mitz say, "...and I would like to introduce this year's student body president, James Merchant. I'll turn the assembly over to him."

In an instant, the seniors shattered the quiet reverie with cheering and whooping and whistling. A mere prologue to the next act, in which an enormous boy jumped out of his front-row seat and leapfrogged onto the stage. We could hear Mr. Mitz saying, "Mr. Merchant, the stairs next time," as much to all of us as to Merchant, but we now knew that that was the only way to get onto the stage. In response, the boy gave him a huge, ironic smile, and it was clear that he would never use the stairs. In his hand was an enormous wooden gavel, which he waved at his fans from the stage.

The seniors began shouting, "Merchant, Merchant, Merchant," over and over until Merchant held up his tan arms, which had at least six yellow *LiveStrong* bracelets on them. He bowed a few times, gestured to them to quiet down, and then banged the gavel up and down on the podium until the chanting stopped. I could tell that he loved this, banging his gavel right in sync with their chanting. He was like the ringleader of a three-ring circus, confident about bringing out lions and tigers and certain that every trick would thrill the audience.

I could not imagine standing on that stage in front of this crowd. I was astonished by his confidence, and I could not stop staring at him. I had never seen anyone like him in my life.

The St. Stephen's teachers lined the walls of the auditorium like security personnel, complete with their own blue blazers and stern expressions, but they seemed to relax when James Merchant took the stage. He could control the crowd better than they could, and everyone seemed to know that.

Once the room had quieted down and the rhythmic pounding had stopped, Merchant stretched his huge body over the podium and leaned way down on his forearms as if he were planning to engage in a private conversation with each of us. "Well, hello, boys. I mean, gentlemen. How are you? Thank you for coming back to school. You look lovely, Tommy," he said, looking straight at a boy who had an enormous mound of curly brown hair burying his eyes and even part of his nose. He was slumped down in his seat in the middle of the senior section. "Yes, you do. And your hair … fantastic!" He smiled and winked at his friend, who shook his head like a dog that has just gotten out of a pool. The senior next to Tommy rumpled the huge mound of hair.

Then Merchant scanned the room and waved at a couple of teachers on one of the far walls before continuing. "This will be a year of growth and change and all sorts of stupendous accomplishments for all of us. We need to take risks, push ourselves, climb higher than we've climbed ever before, and never forget to be in dress code at all times! Such sartorial splendor!" He came out from behind the podium and struck a pose, then looked over and winked at Mr. Mitz, who nodded at him with one eyebrow slightly raised.

"Remember, *we* are special. We are all, every last one of us, *very* special! We're St. Stephen's boys—St. Stephen's *gentlemen*. If two roads diverge in the woods, and it's a snowy evening and all that, take the path that's well worn. Why go where nobody has gone before? We'd have to shovel a lot of sh...snow. And, remember, whatever we do in life, we are products of the greatest school in New York City...no, make that the United States of America...no, make that the world! We go to the greatest school in the world. Don't forget that! And," he added, pausing for a minute, "long live the Tribal Brotherhood!" His last words whipped the group into a frenzy again.

I was now familiar with the script and did my part, stomping and shouting along with every other boy in that packed room. Then Merchant raised his hands high above his head, as if he had just won the Tour de France, before bringing them down to the podium again and pounding the gavel to demand silence.

He smiled at us and winked. "Thank you. Now...are there any announcements? Come right on down, boys!"

At first I didn't realize that he was joking, mocking all those adults who are always telling kids about roads diverging or taking risks or reaching for the stars and scaling the highest mountains and all that. And I wasn't sure whether this was the best school in the world or not. Was it possible that it was? Did I go to the *best* school in the world? If it weren't the best school, why would this guy pretend that it was? Or claim it was? Hadn't Mr. Mitz basically said the same thing? Jesus, how could *I* be at the best school in the world?

At my middle school graduation, one of our teachers had read the Robert Frost poem about the two roads, so I knew it was an important poem. Besides, Robert Frost was famous—the prize I'd received for being the best language arts student was *The Collected Works of Robert Frost.* Perhaps James Merchant didn't like that poem? It had never crossed my mind that I might not like a poem by a famous poet. Why else would Merchant tell everyone to take the well-traveled road? That was the opposite of what my teacher had said. Robert Frost looked so big and powerful on the front of my book, all that white hair and that big face covered in lines. He was famous. Who was I? This was my first day at St. Stephen's and I hadn't attended one class yet, but already I was learning things.

4

My first class of the day was English. No more language arts—this was high school. What the difference was I didn't know, but I did know from my schedule that freshman English was in Room 442. I followed the pack of freshmen shoving its way out of the auditorium and hoped that some of them were going to Room 442.

After we climbed what seemed like hundreds of stairs, we arrived at a room with a large round table in the center. One of the stout, gray ladies beckoned us in. "Come in, boys. Find a seat. This is freshman English. I'm Ms. Wright. Let's get started!"

The room was nothing like the classrooms in my middle school, where the desks were bolted to the floor and arranged in straight rows. There we had been assigned seats, which changed only when someone got in trouble. Here everyone sat around one big round table. It was like a dinner table, only much larger. Big and wooden, kind of King Arthurish. It was impossible to hide in the back, yet there was no way I was going to sit up front.

Apparently other guys had the same idea, since they went for chairs as far away from the teacher as possible. But Ms. Wright directed a couple of the boys to take seats at the front of the table, right on either side of where she was standing by the board. "Don't be afraid! Come right on up. These are the best seats in the house," she said, smiling as she gestured toward the chairs next to her. Best seats, ha. Not only would she be right there, right on top of me and able to see my every move, but everyone else could look at me. Every time anybody looked at her, he'd be staring at me, too.

I slunk down in my seat, which was way over on the left side of the table, pretty far from where she was. It was close to the door; that might also be good. If I got any more nervous, I really might throw up. I sat there like a stone and stared at an empty page in my notebook. All around me kids were talking to each other, joking about stuff. I focused like hell on that lined piece of white paper. I was staring so hard at the lines that they got all blurry and started to move around, so I started staring at the wooden tabletop instead. Christ, being new was horrible.

The chairs next to me remained empty until two late-comers showed up. One of them looked like everybody else, kind of baggy but still fresh in his new back-to-school clothes, but the other boy was the sloppiest kid I had ever seen. While almost everybody (except for me) wore baggy pants, his were bigger and baggier—the legs were so large he could have fit a small child inside. When he walked, they got tangled in each other, and it was a wonder he didn't get his foot caught in all those yards of fabric and fall down. My mother would have had many things to say about those pants. She hated baggy pants on kids—hence the reason I wasn't wearing them, even though I wished that I were. Everyone else was.

And while almost everybody (including me) had the requisite tie loosened around his neck, this boy's was even looser—the knot was in the middle of his chest. But what stood out most were his shoes: once upon a time they had been expensive leather sneakers, but had since become the dirtiest, smelliest shoes I had ever seen. They reeked. Even boys across the room wrinkled up their noses when he came crashing into the room. Neither sneaker had laces, and when he walked, the shoes slapped on and off his feet like flip-flops—and he wasn't wearing socks.

He didn't seem to care that he was late and made a big entrance, shouting "Howdy" and waving at the teacher as he shuffled over to the chair next to me. He dropped the dirty plastic bag he was carrying on the ground next to his chair—he didn't have a huge backpack like everyone else.

"You must be Alex Singleton," the teacher said to him.

"Yes, ma'am, I am. But please, if you don't mind, call me Alexander from now on. I'm going by Alexander now— you know, high school and all." As he spoke, he adjusted the knot on his tie and raised his eyebrows slightly, cocking his head and giving her a knowing look. His comfort with the teacher astonished me, although I couldn't figure out whether he was serious or trying to be funny or what. Nobody was laughing, although a few boys had amused looks on their faces.

"Alexander, yes, certainly," she said, making a note on a sheet in front of her as if this name-change business was standard practice, part of the drill. "Does anybody else have a name he would like to be called, other than what's on my list?"

A boy on the other side of the room raised his hand. "My Christian name is Matthew, but would you call me Peeves from now on?"

Was this a joke?

"Yes, of course," our teacher said as she wrote again on her sheet. She had been through this before. Nothing seemed to surprise or annoy her. I sensed that other boys were thinking about changing their names, as a few whispered to their neighbors and then giggled. I realized that right now I, too, could change my name. Nobody knew me. Nobody knew anything about me. Right now I could become somebody else, somebody with a simple, ordinary American name. I could become anybody I wanted to be.

The trouble was that I had no idea who I wanted to be, who I could become, or anything like that. I wanted to fit in, and I wanted to become a St. Stephen's gentleman, but I didn't know yet what that required. I also suspected that if I raised my hand to speak, I would throw up.

My hands, clasped together in my lap, were clammy. Every few seconds I squeezed them together as hard as I could, trying to release energy. I had read somewhere about doing that when you're nervous, like before you make a speech or something. Nothing helped, though. I couldn't speak; I couldn't change my name or anything else. And the stench of those sneakers wasn't helping matters.

I glanced down at the floor and realized that from where I was sitting, I could see inside Alexander's plastic bag. There were two books about chess, something by an author named Gogol, the *New York Times*, and three Spider-Man comic books. Also a bottle of chocolate milk and a package of small, white-powdered doughnuts.

"Ma'am," Alexander said without raising his hand. "Would it be okay if I ate my breakfast? I was rushed this morning and haven't had time to eat." He gave her this big smile. I could just picture what this kid would look like eating those powdered doughnuts.

"Alexander, you may not eat in here. I'm sorry you're hungry. Perhaps there's time later in your schedule to go to the dining hall, the only place where food is allowed in the school." She smiled at him, then turned her attention back to the rest of us.

"Let's start. Would someone read the lines on the poster over there?" She pointed toward a poster on the wall behind where I was sitting. It was one of those posters I sometimes saw on the bus or the subway; in fact, there were a bunch of them on the walls. *Poetry in Motion*, the posters said at the top. I read them sometimes when I was on the subway.

Nobody raised his hand, and Ms. Wright looked down at the attendance list.

Oh shit, I thought. Please don't call on me. Please don't make me read in front of the class. As I sat there wishing that the carpet would swallow up me and my chair and the horrible feeling inside me, I heard Alexander say, "Oh come on, fellows! What are you—shy on the first day of school? I'll read, Ms. Wright."

"Thank you, Alexander."

He turned around in his chair a bit, and his eyes scanned the poster. "Oh, it's *Romeo and Juliet*—one of my favorite Shakespearean tragedies. Did you see it at the Public last year? Ms. Wright, what do you think of the Baz Luhrmann film? Claire Danes—vah-vah-vah-vooooooom! I'm all for contemporary versions of the bard's works, but there were ... "

"Alexander, please read." Ms. Wright gestured toward the wall.

He cleared his throat about six times and started to

read in this high-pitched, squeaky voice: "*Come*, night, *come*, Romeo, *come*, thou day in night..." Every time he said the word "come," his voice became louder and higher and totally crazy, and a bunch of guys howled with laughter. Even I smiled a little.

"Alexander," Ms. Wright said, and her voice had a slight sharpness to it. "There's no need to change your voice, even if you are playing Juliet." Then she added in a high-pitched voice that sounded like Minnie Mouse, "No woman or girl sounds like that, and no need to dwell on certain words..." Everyone cracked up, even me. Her voice went back to normal and she said, "Just use your regular voice. And, the rest of you need to be *silent*." She looked once around the room, and all the talking and laughing stopped.

Alexander continued, this time in his regular voice. "'For thou wilt lie upon the wings of night, whiter than new snow on a raven's back...'" He kept reading and I tried to follow along, but my brain felt all tangled up, even kind of frozen-like, and the words weren't fitting together into anything that made much sense.

Right after he read the last line, Ms. Wright said, "So..." Then she paused and looked around at all of us before adding, "Why do we need poetry?" She looked around the room again, then turned and wrote her question on the board.

I took a few peeks at some of the other kids, trying to see whether they knew what she was talking about. A couple of them had their hands raised. I could see one boy a few seats over playing tic-tac-toe with his neighbor. I heard a little rustling and looked over to see that Alexander was opening the doughnut package inside of the dirty plastic bag. He had peeled back part of the package and was now licking some powdered sugar off his fingers.

When she turned around to face us, he raised his hand. "Ma'am, poetry lets us be poetic. Prose is good, too, and sometimes we can be a little poetic in our prose—you know, a simile here and there, symbolic stuff, what have you. But when we're wooing the ladies, we need poetry, like good ole Romeo. May he rest in peace." He crossed himself when he finished speaking, and some boys snickered. The way he talked was mostly easy to understand, although I didn't know what prose was.

"Yes." Ms. Wright smiled, then added, "Although I am curious as to how many of you are 'wooing the ladies.' Nevertheless, the idea that poetic language enables us to express our deepest emotions is critical." She paused for a moment, then asked, "What's the dominant image in this passage?" She looked across the room, away from Alexander, who took this opportunity to dig back into the doughnut package. He also started to loosen the top on the chocolate milk. I struggled to concentrate: my attention was divided between the discussion and the secretive activities next to me—the doughnut drama, taking place in a dirty plastic bag on the floor of our classroom.

I was amazed as well. Ms. Wright had told him not to eat, yet he was eating. Then, when he wasn't eating, he was leading the class discussion. I was sitting there sick with worry about just being in the room, silently doing nothing and hoping nobody was going to call attention to me—especially our teacher—and here was this guy, Alexander, who didn't have a worry in the world. He was having a blast.

A kid on the other side of the room raised his hand. He had been sitting in front of me in the assembly hall—I remembered him because he was so tall that he had partially blocked my view of the stage. Ms. Wright called on him, and he said, "Shakespeare uses contrasts here to reveal the night—the juxtaposition of the whiteness of 'new snow' with the back of a black raven. But that's just one of the images." He paused for a second, then continued. "What stands out to me are the irony and the foreshadowing. We all know how the play ends, and here we see Juliet's early reference to Romeo's death. But, ironically, it's a beautiful and alluring image."

It was? What was he talking about? He spoke with certainty, and his statements were full of fancy language. He sounded like some of my dad's friends from Columbia, where my dad was a professor. It wasn't just the kid's height that made him stand out. Even though he was tall, if you could see just his face, he looked like a baby—his skin was so smooth. But when he spoke it was weird, like trapped inside of him was some old professor.

"You're right," Ms. Wright said as she jotted on the board

an abbreviated version of what he had said. "Remind me of your name. You're new to St. Stephen's, yes?"

"I'm Henry Steel. I am new. I came from St. Sebastian's." Henry spoke deliberately, and the way he said his old school's name almost made me think he had an English accent. I was astonished by how comfortable he, too, was in this setting and with his ideas, which our teacher seemed to love.

While she was focused on Henry, Alexander leaned over to the side of his chair and took a sip of chocolate milk. A boy across the room snickered, and Ms. Wright suddenly turned her attention from Henry to the boy who had laughed and then to the target of that laughter. Her head whipped around fast, tracing the line of small exchanges.

In a flash, she was next to me and Alexander, digging into his plastic bag and removing the doughnuts and milk. She took them over to the trash can and threw them in with such force that we all heard the thud of the milk container against the metal bottom of the can.

"Alexander," she said in an even, clear tone, "you may *not* eat in here. The dining hall is the *only* place where food is allowed in the school."

Alexander looked slightly dismayed. But it had all taken place so fast, and she had remained so calm, that he was still trying to figure out what had happened. Out of the corner of my eye, I could see him chewing on the cap of a pen while he made little doodles of doughnuts in his notebook.

I managed to get through the period without being called on. It was almost as though Ms. Wright knew I would drop dead—bam—just fall right out of my chair and die right then and there right in the midst of that talk about poetry and juxtapositions and foreshadowing and all that. She called on lots of other guys, though. Most of them didn't have too much to say. Nobody else said anything about irony or stuff like that, but some of them were smart. What stood out most was how damn comfortable they were with all this, just sitting around talking about poetry and Shakespeare.

There was this one kid, though—Mark Zimmer— who didn't know anything and didn't care. When Ms. Wright called on him, he had his chair tilted back on two legs and was leaning against the wall. On his face were mirrored sunglasses, with big white frames that had rhinestones all over them. He had a bunch of gold chains on and his pants were big and baggy, of course. He wasn't big; in fact, he was small, kind of tiny even, and it was like he was buried under all his clothes and chains. When she called on him, it was as though she were moving in on him, swooping in. But before asking him about some lines in a poem, she said, "Take your sunglasses off, put your chair flat on the floor, and get out a notebook."

He lowered his chair to the floor, pushed his sunglasses up onto his head, looked around, and then, in response to her question, said kind of slowly, "I have no idea, no clue." Then he shrugged his shoulders and got this bored look on his face, as if thinking about this stuff was going to put him to sleep. One of the other boys muttered under his breath, "Zimmer ... " and a bunch of them rolled their eyes.

As I sat there wondering what was wrong with him, I tried to peek over at him. I had no idea where he was looking, because of the huge dark glasses, which he'd put back on about five minutes after Ms. Wright asked him to take them off. I hadn't ever seen a white boy dressed like that.

I was kind of lost in thinking about how he didn't care what our teacher thought while I was so worried about everyone and everything, and just getting this feeling of doom inside me because I didn't know anything, when I heard Ms. Wright saying, "Go, go, go." She had suddenly noticed that she had run over the end of the period. We all quickly gathered our stuff and headed toward the door. "Run to your next class!" she called.

Despite her instructions, Alexander lumbered slowly away from the table and stopped at the trash can. From the front of the room, Ms. Wright called out, "Don't even think about it, Alexander. Go to your next class!" He shuffled off at that point, after a final forlorn glance at his food.

5

At lunch, I discovered how much most of the kids in my classes hated Mark Zimmer. I went through the lunch line as slowly as I could, trying to put off what I would have to face: I had nobody to sit with. Until today, I had always brought my lunch to school. None of the kids I hung out with at my old school ate the cafeteria food, or, if they did, they spent the whole time complaining about it. Here everybody ate the cafeteria food, and they didn't even call the place a cafeteria—it was a dining hall. And they didn't have those regular school trays either, the one with the different compartments for all the food groups.

They had the special trays that I loved, with the school's Latin motto right in the middle of them.

There were all kinds of food choices in the dining hall. Three hot entrees (one vegetarian), homemade soup, and baskets filled with rolls and muffins. There was also a huge salad bar, a deli spread, and bagels and cream cheese. You could have as much milk or juice as you wanted, and they had three different desserts and a frozen yogurt machine. It was like a food court in there.

I got in the line and was kind of slyly checking out all of the food, trying not to meet anybody's eyes as we inched along. When I got to the hot food, I filled my tray with a plate of macaroni and cheese; a small, very white and round dinner roll; two pats of butter; and two glasses of milk. I gathered up all this food because I needed something to do. I wasn't hungry—what the hell was I going to do with all this food? There was enough on my tray to feed my whole family. Then I stopped at the salad bar and created this big old salad of practically every little chopped-up vegetable in the world.

All that time, as I agonized over the arrangement of sliced-up vegetables, not one guy called out to me, "Hey Mauricio, come sit with us." Nothing. Nada. No one said "Hi" or "Hey" or "Excuse me, can I get to the tomatoes?" or even just reached the hell over me to get some cucumbers or something. No one looked at me or noticed me. I started to hate them all. Bastards. They were all so goddamn confident and comfortable. Most of them had been eating lunch in this dining hall since they were five, and they walked in like they owned the place and couldn't care less if some new guy had nobody to sit with.

I spotted an empty seat at the end of one of the long tables. There were some younger kids sitting there, over on the other end of the table. I walked over, sat down quietly, and started to eat. I focused on my food, although I was certain those kids were looking at me. I was sure one of them said, "Who's that guy?" and gave a weird look to his friends. I locked my eyes on that little dinner roll and thought about how much I hated being new. There was an enormous chasm—wider than the damn Grand Canyon—between how I had been imagining myself at St. Stephen's all summer long and how I felt now.

All summer I'd sat in my bedroom, reading the school's website and picturing myself hanging out with the kids in the photos—all casual and cool, a bunch of guys gathered around some math book, everyone looking happy and nice, figuring out some equation or something. Now here I was in the fancy old dining hall, sitting all by myself and trying to act like it was no big deal. Back when I was busy falling in love with the image of myself at St. Stephen's, I'd never stopped to think that maybe I would have no one to sit with at lunch.

The table next to mine was filled with a bunch of guys from my classes. Every so often I took my eyes off the dinner roll, which was dusted with flour on the top and reminded me of Alexander's doughnuts, and peeked over at them. They were playing a game with a folded up piece of paper, a little triangle-like thing, which they flicked up and down the long table. One guy sat at each end of the table and created a goalpost by stretching his hands out, putting his pointer fingers together and extending his thumbs upwards.

"That's out, asshole," one of them shouted at the boy who had asked Ms. Wright to call him Peeves.

"Fuck you, man. Put on your glasses, Harrison, you blind bat!"

"Take the shot over already," another guy said, in a bored voice.

"Hey, here comes Zimmer." They all looked over at Mark Zimmer, who was walking toward their table.

"That dickwad."

Zimmer walked up, holding a tray of food. "Move over," he said to one of the guys. The boy didn't move, so Zimmer set his tray down on the empty table and said it again. "Move over." All the boys at the table had stopped playing the game. Zimmer's tray was sitting right in the middle of their field, calling a temporary halt to their flicking the folded-up paper up and down while swearing at each other.

In every class that morning, these guys had found ways to give Zimmer a hard time. Nobody would lend him a pencil when he needed one, they rolled their eyes any time he said anything, and they muttered insults about him under their breath. But now he wanted to eat lunch with them. He was nuts. I sure as hell wasn't ever going to sit with those guys. But right then all I did was sit there silently, praying like hell that Zimmer wasn't going to turn around and sit down with me. I got all focused on my roll again. Then I heard one of them say, "Hey, Zimmer, is it true your mother's doing it with Mitz?"

Then I heard him say, "Fuck you guys. Mitzy's dick isn't big enough for my mother." Out of the corner of my eye I saw him grab his pants, and he said, "Oh yeah," and kind of thrust his hips forward. The other guys smirked and shook their heads. Zimmer paused for a second and looked around the room quickly, then said, "Fucking move over. I have information you want."

Then it got all quiet and everything, and the next thing I knew he was sitting down, kind of right in the middle of the group, and they were all huddled up around him. I had no idea what they were doing, but I was ready to get out of there.

As I was dumping all my food in the trash, I looked over at the table again. They were still all leaned in close. At the time, I couldn't understand what they could want from Zimmer, why they had finally moved over and let him sit down, or why he would want to be with them. But there they all were, sitting together like a pack of wolves all set on eating some dead animal that Zimmer had dragged over.

6

I walked down the stairs and headed back into the foyer area. I had discovered earlier that everybody left his backpack in the foyer during lunch. Following the crowd, I'd thrown my bag into the pile that was forming. Now the pile was about five times bigger, and I had to dig through tons of packs to find mine on the bottom.

While I was doing this, I heard someone call out, "Yo, dude!" I looked around and there was Alexander—sitting on one of the long wooden benches with a pizza box, the *New York Times* open in front of him. In his hand was a large soda. He waved me over.

"Hey," he said as he reached out his hand to shake mine. His hand and his face were greasy, and I could see large grease spots on the pages of the newspaper and his tie, but I shook his hand. "Alexander. Alexander Singleton," he continued. "But you know that. We were sitting next to each other in English."

"Yeah ... I'm Mauricio," I said, nodding my head up and down, until I thought about how dumb I must have looked and stopped nodding.

"Seven-letter word for 'modern business equipment' ... any ideas?" Alexander chewed on the end of a ballpoint pen as he stared down at the paper spread out around him.

"Uh ... what?" I sputtered.

He looked me up and down, and I wondered what he was thinking, but I said nothing. Other guys were starting to come into the foyer and dig through the enormous pile of backpacks. "Mauricio ... that's some fancy name. Where are you from?"

"Uh ... my dad's Cuban, and my mom's French, but I'm a New Yorker."

"Mets or Yankees?"

"Mets."

"Ah, Mauricio, you're killing me! Please. Now, let's see ... " He paused for a moment and looked up toward the ceiling. "Hmmm ... should I root for the franchise that has won more world championships than any other professional sports team in the world, or root for a team that plays at Shea Stadium in clown outfits. Hmmm ... let me think it over and get back to you." He went back to chewing on the end of his pen.

I didn't say anything, but I was starting to smile a little.

"Now, look here, Mauricio, you're gonna be okay. I'll introduce you to some guys." Alexander looked around, but the only person who was still in the foyer, sitting on one of the other wooden benches reading, was Henry Steel, the boy who seemed to know as much as our teachers. In every class that morning he'd had something to say—something that I couldn't understand and that had made our teachers practically drool.

"Yo, Buns! Buns of Steel!" Henry looked around and gave Alexander a raised eyebrow. "Hey, come over here. I want you to meet a friend of mine."

Henry closed his book, stood up, and walked over to Alexander and me. "Having a little snack, *Alexander?*" It was clear that these guys knew each other from somewhere.

"Well, I lost the doughnuts," Alexander said in a sad voice, then sniffed dramatically. "But listen here—Buns, this is Mauricio ... Mauricio ... what?"

"Londoño."

"Okay, Mauricio Londoño. He's Cuban."

"Nice to meet you," Henry said, extending his hand toward me. I had never shaken so many hands in one day. I mumbled, "Nice to know you" or something.

"Where did you go to school before St. Stephen's?" Henry asked.

"PS 245."

"Really?" Henry sounded surprised.

"Yeah," I said quietly. I could feel my face turning red. The tips of my ears felt warm.

"Buns ... please! Buns doesn't get out much ... although there were those dancing classes back in fifth grade. Let me tell you, Mauricio," Alexander said as he looked over at me, "Buns tore up the rug. But it's been downhill ever since ... " He sighed as he reached up and patted Henry on the arm. Henry smirked. "But Buns, do tell, how is beautiful Biz?"

"Elizabeth?"

"Elizabeth, light of my life, my soul. E-liz-a-beth. Biz, Liz, Liza, Eliza, Lizzy, dear sweet beautiful Biz. You know, Buns, your sister ... the one who does get out. Your twin ... the one who lives in your apartment, the one you shared the womb with. Good ole beautiful Biz. Is she still dating that idiot George Wilkinson? Man, he's impressive ... yeah? He's on steroids ... that must be it ... or maybe his Ritalin dosage is off?"

Henry laughed and said, "I don't keep up with Elizabeth. Everything changes too quickly. I'll give her your regards. But, Alexander, what did you do to your tie?" Alexander looked down at his tie and then brought it right up to his mouth and used it like a napkin to wipe away pizza grease and crumbs. Henry laughed again, then turned to me. "Nice to meet you, Mauricio," he said as he walked away and headed up the stairs.

Alexander picked up a slice of pizza and took a big bite, then slurped his soda. "Look here, Mauricio—you mind if I change that? Manny...that'll work. Look here, Manny, you'll get used to this place. It's not too bad. I've been here for years and look at me!" He held out his arms and gestured at the mess that surrounded him. "Good old St. Stephen's—sound mind in a sound body." He took a huge bite of pizza. I was nodding again as I started to head toward the stairs. "Hey...you want some advice?" he called out.

"Okay," I said, not sure what this guy would advise me on—white powdered doughnuts, the *New York Times*, smelly sneakers?

"Plastics..." He started to laugh right when he said this. I must have looked confused, but then he said, "No, really, here's some advice: go out for wrestling. Great sport. Check it out this winter. I don't actually wrestle myself; I'm more of a team manager of sorts. And I do some recruiting, you know—help out with building the team, scouting for prospects, that kind of thing. But wrestling is the best. Hand-to-hand combat. Classic. Oldest sport in the world. The Greeks were down with it—big-time male bodies and all." He stretched his arms out, flexed his muscles, then winked and smiled at me before continuing. "It's in the *Bible*, man. You know, Jacob wrestling that angel..." He held his hands out in front of himself, crouched over a bit, and moved his arms around. I had no idea what he was doing; later, after my first wrestling practice, I realized that he was imitating a wrestler's opening stance. "Think about it, Manny. You're here with all these guys, might as well be down with the Tribal Brotherhood and all that good stuff...oh yeah...wrestling is the balls."

"Thanks," I said hesitantly, and started to walk toward the steps. It was almost time for biology—although Alexander didn't look like he was anywhere near finished with either his picnic or the newspaper, which was spread out all over the bench and the floor.

7

By the end of the day, I knew that Alexander Single-ton, Henry Steel, Matthew "Peeves" Rosenblatt, Scott Harrison, Mark Zimmer, and George Wilkinson were in all of my classes. Henry and I were the only ones who were new to St. Stephen's; the other boys had been together since kindergarten. They were like brothers in how they insulted each other and joked around. But it was obvious, even to me, that they weren't all friends.

Alexander joked with them and came up with snappy comebacks for their constant remarks about his clothes and shoes, but he didn't seem to care what they thought.

At one point he even took off one of those filthy shoes and threw it right at George's head. When they teased him about Ms. Wright and wooing the ladies, he just took the newspaper out of his dirty plastic bag and started to read it.

By the end of the first day, I had seen over and over how desperate Mark Zimmer was to be with some of these guys. He trailed after them when they left one class and headed to the next. They never waited for him. When we were all standing in the hallway, waiting for a class, he tried to edge his way into their conversations, but he barely hovered on the perimeter. They ridiculed every idea he tossed out about music or sports, yet he persisted in trying to get their attention. Any kind of attention was better than none, it seemed.

But there was something he had that they all wanted. They'd basically told him to fuck off at lunch; then the whole thing had turned, and they huddled together talking about something. I was so naïve at the time that I couldn't imagine what it was that this guy had.

Almost from the minute I'd first seen Zimmer and his huge, rhinestone-encrusted sunglasses, I hated him too. There was something about him that was repulsive. But all I knew then was that I planned to stay as far away from him as possible. At one point during our first math class, where I had ended up sitting next to him, he turned to me and said loudly, "Yo, man, got a pencil I can borrow?"

A cold, creepy feeling came over me, and I was sure that all those guys were watching me, all twisted around in their seats doggedly gauging my every move, trying to see what I would do. Of course, nobody was paying any attention. I looked down at my desk, shook my head slightly, and said in a small voice, "Sorry."

It was easy to see that Peeves, Harrison, and Wilkinson were the inner circle, the power brokers in the class, but within the trio Wilkinson was the boss, Harrison and Peeves his henchmen. That was even clear from how they walked around together: Wilkinson in the center with Peeves and Harrison on either side.

All day, nobody went after Wilkinson about anything. He was sacred, it seemed. And he didn't even look like a ninth grader—he was as tall as Henry but not as scrawny. He was big and muscular—maybe he was on steroids?—and his voice was low and deep and commanded attention. I got the feeling right away that I didn't want to be on this guy's shit list. And even though I wouldn't have admitted it, he looked cool. I kind of wanted to figure out how he did it, how he drew such attention and moved in that big body so effortlessly.

Harrison, however, was fat. His friends joked about diets and husky-sized jeans and super-sizing everything. Peeves was Jewish, so they'd ask him where his yarmulke was or why Jews read backwards or anything else they could come up with. Nothing was sacred. Someone was always going to do someone else's mother or sister, especially if the mother was hot—as opposed to the fat ugly ones, whom they didn't hesitate to describe in disgusting details.

I hoped these guys would never see my mother—who I guessed was hot because she wasn't fat—but she was my mother, for God's sake. I sure as hell didn't want them to find out that she was French, especially with all they were saying about the new French and Spanish teacher.

Before the end of my first day at St. Stephen's, I had been told that George Wilkinson was the smartest boy in the class *and* the best athlete. That was like some kind of common knowledge. Guys talked about him in reverential voices in the locker room while we changed for PE. He didn't do PE, since he played varsity soccer. Because of that, he was also the only one in our class who was exempt from the seniors' teasing. They needed him on the team. He just seemed to glide through that first day, his two henchmen on either side of him, poised to laugh at or agree with anything he said.

I just wanted to steer clear of all of them—I didn't want them to know anything about me. I promised myself I would lie low and not give them any ammunition, just stay the hell out of the line of fire. I had been so eager to go to St. Stephen's; I had believed the admissions letter that described how everyone "couldn't wait to welcome me into the St. Stephen's family." Here I was now, practically running for cover like a scared mouse. I had proudly put on my little dress-code outfit that morning, my father cheerfully helping me with my tie—which I had discovered, on entering the building, had to be worn loose around the neck. That was easy to accomplish, but loosening my tie did nothing to ease my deep feeling of not belonging.

By the end of that first day, I was exhausted. Who would have imagined that trying to fade into the walls was so demanding? Perhaps it was the low-level terror that accompanied my every move, and that feeling of being some kind of uninvited guest, that were so damn tiring. By five o'clock I had a backpack filled with a billion books to lug home and homework for every one of my new classes, all neatly copied down in my St. Stephen's planbook complete with the fancy Latin motto emblazoned on its cover. And I had just gone through a weight-training drill in PE. I stunk from sweating, and I was starving.

I sat down on a bench right by the front door to rest before making my way to the bus stop. I was like a deflated balloon, just some floppy old rubbery version of my former self—my perky, eager, idiotic former self.

Sitting on the bench with me were two lower-school kids, maybe seven or eight years old. They were trading magic cards and talking about school. At one point I had been a huge fan of magic cards. I was happy to see that they cared as much as I had about the Time Spiral cards. At least I had something in common with someone at this place. I planned to sit there for just a few minutes before heading out, but then I couldn't drag myself away from their conversation.

They were in the midst of a debate about why girls couldn't go to St. Stephen's. "They aren't smart enough, and, you know, this is the best school," one said confidently to the other, who smiled. He liked the idea. Right above them were all these pictures of old white guys, dozens of them, all serious and scary-looking with their grim faces and bald shiny heads. Everyone here seemed to think this was the best school in the city. But after spending the day continually praying that no teacher would call on me, and pretty much cowering in the corner, I didn't feel smart. In fact, I felt stupid; I had no idea about imagery or symbolism or any of that stuff.

Just then, I heard a rapping on one of the big glass front doors to the right of where we were sitting. A large man was knocking, gesturing to the two boys to come outside.

"Come on," one of the boys said. "There's my dad. Let's go."

The father stood in front of the school, his quick hand gestures at the boys revealing his impatience. His phone was glued to his ear, and he never once stopped talking during the time that he waved at them and ushered them into the big, black car. When his son pulled on his jacket sleeve and tried to get his attention, the father never looked down—he just stuffed him in the car, then climbed in himself, yacking away on that fancy silver phone.

This man, in his suit with his cell phone cemented to his ear, could not have been more different from my father, who didn't even like talking on the phone in our apartment and refused to get a cell phone. Why would he want to talk on the phone when he was outside? Or on the bus? He had to be the last person in New York City who used pay phones, when he could find one that worked. My dad was like a funny antique. He just didn't care about electronics, no matter how much I told him about cool stuff.

I slowly made my way over to the bus stop on Broadway, where another St. Stephen's kid and a woman with three bags of groceries were waiting. The kid nodded at me but said nothing. He made no effort to talk to me, so I didn't talk to him.

As I waited for the bus, I thought about what it would be like to have a driver. No more waiting at the bus stop. No more crowded subway trains. No more standing up in a hot, smelly crowd. I pictured myself sitting in the back seat of a big, black car. My uncle had a beautiful Mercedes, and the seats were made of the smoothest leather I'd ever felt. I loved sitting up front in the passenger's seat, which had its own heater. My uncle sometimes took me out. He was young and cool, and he let me do stuff my parents never did.

It was hard to believe he was my dad's younger brother, because my dad didn't own a car. He didn't even have a driver's license. He hated driving. He *liked* sitting on the bus, watching the city pass by or reading a book. Sometimes he took a taxi, but he loved the bus, even though it stopped every two blocks and took forever. He just wanted to see the city, watch people, take his time. That was my dad.

I was imagining myself sitting in the back of one of

those cars—the driver up front and me in the back, talking on my cell phone or watching DVDs—when the bus pulled up. It was packed with people, and I had to stand until 86th Street.

I finally got a seat next to an old man, who refused to move over and instead turned his legs into the aisle and pointed toward the window seat. I squeezed past him, after hoisting my backpack over him and onto the floor in front of the seat. After I sat down, I started to feel as though I might never be able to stand up again. Even a hard plastic seat on a crowded bus, with me squeezed against the window by a large old man, my feet propped up on the huge backpack on the floor, felt restful. I couldn't do anything but sit there.

But then that whole first day and all the dreary details started popping into my mind. I had been happy in the morning, before I left my apartment. It was finally the first day of school, which I'd been looking forward to ever since my admissions visit months before. One thing I'd remembered vividly from that admissions visit was the noise. Everywhere I went, voices had boomed—up and down the staircases, bounding through the cramped hallways, bouncing off the walls in the classrooms. The voices and the backpacks crowded the stairwells, moving as one enormous body—one pushing, flailing, backslapping, jostling, shoving body. It seemed as if at any moment the walls would burst open, the roof would fly off, and all those boys would soar straight up into the sky. Yet I'd loved it all and was eager to be there, amidst all that noise and energy.

Now I sat on that hard bus seat, sacked out, so beat from navigating that crazy place and all those bodies and noise and the gargantuan backpacks. Some of the bags were bigger than the kids who tried to maneuver the narrow stairs under their bulky weight. They looked like the Sherpas in those pictures of climbers trying to ascend Everest—human pack mules.

I sat on that bus and imagined the roof flying off the school and everyone soaring away. Those backpacks would crash right down to the ground, creating an enormous heap of abandoned biology and geometry textbooks. Here and there books like *Learn to Read Latin* and *The Great Gatsby* would lie, spines broken and pages rumpled and ripped, but there wouldn't be one boy anywhere. All those boys would just float off into the huge blue Manhattan sky, like balloons some little kid let go of. Maybe that's what happens when you fill a school with eight hundred boys. It generates explosive energy.

Maybe I should have known better. My friend Leo had tried to warn me for weeks. I had bumped into him that morning, when I was walking to the subway. He and his dad kind of warned me again.

"Mauricio! Hey!" I turned around and there was Leo. He lived in my building and had been my friend since we were babies.

"Wow! Look at you," his dad added. "Are you heading

to Wall Street?" He started to laugh as he reached over and pretended to pick some lint off my blazer.

"Yeah, what's with the tie? What's that about?" Leo was looking me up and down.

"It's the dress code," I said quietly. Even though Leo and I had been friends forever, he got mad when I decided to go to St. Stephen's. His parents even asked my parents whether they were worried about putting me in a school with so many rich kids.

"You look like some kind of a weird man, like you're wearing your dad's clothes or something." Leo looked at me again and wrinkled up his nose, as if I smelled bad.

"Yeah, I guess." I didn't know what to say. For the past few months, I hadn't known whether I wanted to be his friend anymore. He wouldn't stop saying shitty things about St. Stephen's. Leo was going to Bronx Science, and he tried to get me to go there too. Then he got mad and called me a snob when I didn't end up going. Originally we'd talked about both of us going to Stuyvesant, but neither of us got in. I had never said much to Leo about St. Stephen's, but from the minute I visited the school, I knew that was where I wanted to go. Nothing anyone said could have changed my mind. I was even kind of glad when I didn't get in to Stuy.

We'd kept walking along, nobody saying anything. I was happy when we got to the corner of 113th and Broadway. "See you later," I said and kind of waved. I looked over at his dad and gave him a little smile. He smiled back.

"Yeah, see ya." Leo nodded his head at me but didn't look at me. He just kept his eyes down, as if the cement in the sidewalk on Broadway was fascinating. I sort of cared that he didn't like me anymore and that he was being a jerk, but I was pissed about what he'd been saying—like that everyone was gay at that faggot boys' school or that guys would do weird shit in the locker room. My parents said he felt bad, that he was disappointed we weren't going to school together anymore.

Maybe I had been a fool not to stick with Leo, not to go to Bronx Science. Sitting there on that smelly, crowded bus, I remembered how sure I had been that St. Stephen's was the right school for me. Then I started thinking, what if I stayed on the bus? What if I stayed right in my hard, plastic seat after the bus passed my stop? Maybe the bus went all the way up to the George Washington Bridge. Maybe I would go to New Jersey. Just get off the bus and walk across the bridge. Here I was—a student at the famous, the fabulous St. Stephen's School for Boys—and what I wanted to do was walk across the George Washington Bridge and wander around in New Jersey. Never go home.

I knew that when I got home, my mom would want to know everything about my first day—all that stuff about whether I made new friends, what the boys were like, what I ate for lunch, just everything. I was too tired to face all that, and what in the hell would I tell her?

I looked around and wondered where everyone else was going. Everywhere I looked, people seemed deflated, worn out. The skin on the face of the man next to me sagged in folds under his eyes and chin. Maybe he hadn't moved over because it was too much effort.

The woman with the groceries was still standing. She had her bags arranged around her feet and kept adjusting them whenever people wanted to get to the back door. I could see milk and broccoli inside one of the bags, and I wondered whether she was planning to eat broccoli for dinner. I wished that all I had to do was go home, eat dinner, and go to bed. If I thought too much about what had happened, I would start to cry. More than anything, I didn't want to cry.

During several moments of panic that day—when Zimmer had asked me for the pencil; when the biology teacher called on me, and I had nothing to say—a cold, creepy feeling had come over me. Then a hard lump had formed in my throat and made it hard to swallow. I'd fought it—so much that my head hurt. I clenched my teeth and concentrated on not crying. Now I had hours of homework to complete, and that same awful feeling was building inside me. I was hoping my dad could explain the poem Ms. Wright had assigned, something about beauty and art inside an urn of ashes or something like that. Maybe he could tell me what the poem meant. I sure as hell didn't know.

8

By the beginning of October, when the weather was starting to change, I could have my tie knotted and then loosened in a minute or two. Sometimes I didn't even bother untying it when I got home; I lifted it over my head, threw it on a chair, and put it back on the next day. All of my ties had stains on them, but I wouldn't let my mom take them to the cleaners.

I had been at St. Stephen's for more than a month, but I still rarely spoke in class. Most of the kids in my class ignored me. At least I wasn't like Mark Zimmer, whom everyone hated. I was pretty sure that even Ms. Wright couldn't stand Zimmer. He was always late to her class and never had his homework when she came around to collect it. She'd started the term giving him the benefit of the doubt, asking him to turn the assignment in as soon as he found it or to print out another copy and bring it the next day. But after a few weeks, she became impatient. "Don't tell me," she would say when she arrived at his chair, her hand held out for his work, "you can't find your homework." She would sigh loudly and shake her head before moving on to the next student.

Initially he'd talked back, trying to show off in front of us, to let her know he wasn't afraid of her or that he thought she didn't know what she was talking about. During class discussions, he would come up with questions he thought she couldn't answer. But she flattened him verbally, matching every complaint or question he issued with witty and quick responses that led most of the class to laugh. I joined in, and it felt good.

There was a rumor that Ms. Wright met with Zimmer, Mitzy, and Zimmer's parents after the class where she kicked him out.

That was toward the end of September. We had English last period on that day, and the class had gotten off to a bad start when almost everyone had come in about ten minutes late. We were all in a bad mood because our math test had been too hard, and everyone was loudly discussing one of the problems when we entered Ms. Wright's classroom. I was trying to cope with the sick feeling that had come over me as we stomped up the stairs from math to English. I had been confident about the problem everybody was complaining about, but now I knew I'd gotten it wrong.

I had studied all night for the test, had gone over every homework problem with my dad, and now I was sure that I hadn't done well. I couldn't think about anything except how unfair it was that our teacher had made the test so hard. I was fuming, and for once I didn't care what Ms. Wright thought. She did everything she could to help me with her assignments, and I liked her. She didn't put up with bullshit from my classmates, and almost everybody respected her, but that day I didn't give a shit. I wanted to give up. I was struggling so hard to hold back the angry, hot tears I could feel welling up that my head ached. I rubbed both of my eyes hard, as if they were itchy. I was exhausted and angry, and the last thing I wanted to do was talk about another damn poem, which I wouldn't understand anyway.

I felt defeated. I knew the rest of the day would be like every school day: go home, wolf down dinner, and then do hours of homework that was too hard. I let out a long sigh as I sat down.

Ms. Wright was urgently trying to get class going. She was standing in the front of the room, pointing up at the clock. "Find a seat—get your stuff out. We have fewer than thirty minutes for class now. Let's get going." There was no time to waste. There was never any time to waste. There was never a minute simply to relax and do nothing. We were all so deflated that her instructions just hung in the air.

That was when she noticed that Zimmer hadn't arrived. He got extra time on tests because of some kind of learning disability or something, but he was supposed to do that after school. Nobody said anything about where he was. We didn't actually know, but nobody cared.

"Is Mark here today?" Ms. Wright was practically the only person in the school who called him by his first name. Even our other teachers called him Zimmer, and most of my classmates called him everything but his name. When Ms. Wright called him Mark, it was as if she were referring to someone we didn't know.

"He's here but not here," Harrison offered with a little smile, and she made a note on her attendance sheet before asking us to turn to page 43 in our poetry anthologies. She had just posed a question about a Wordsworth poem when Zimmer came crashing into the room.

He wasn't wearing a tie, he was more than twenty minutes late, and he didn't have anything with him—no backpack, notebook, pencil, or poetry book. Nothing. From across the room, I could smell the cigarette smoke that clung to his clothes and skin. He slammed the door shut after having flung it open so hard that the door handle crashed into the wall, and he dropped his body into an empty chair. Then he put his head down on the table in front of him. Everyone in the room knew something disastrous was going to happen. Everyone, that is, except Zimmer—who even if he knew, didn't care.

Ms. Wright waited a moment or two, perhaps wanting to see whether he would offer any explanations for his lateness or lack of books, but he said nothing, just sat there slumped over with his head buried in his hands on the table. What struck me in that moment was that he was doing exactly what I, and probably all of my classmates, felt like doing but wouldn't dare.

"Mark?" she said. No response, so she spoke again but louder. "Mark? What are you doing?"

"Nothing," he mumbled without lifting his head. "Leave me alone."

"Mark, you've missed more than half of class, you have no materials, you are out of dress code, and you are unable to sit up. You need to leave." She waited one more minute. Getting no response, she added in a louder voice, "*Now.*"

We had never seen Ms. Wright kick anybody out of class. Some of the other teachers had kicked kids out, even during the first week of classes—especially the new French and Spanish teacher. The rumor was that everyone was so out of control in her classes that daily bets were wagered about who would get kicked out. I was still kind of sorry that I couldn't take French or Spanish with her, even if her classes were crazy. It would have been great to see her every day.

While most boys respected Ms. Wright, Zimmer was different. She had little patience for him anymore, and he had none for her either. We all watched this tense scene eagerly. There was something thrilling about witnessing someone else get humiliated, as if such an event improved our own standing. We were all his superior in that moment, and that felt good. Even I felt superior to Zimmer.

It was silent in there, and I could hear the heavy breathing of the kid next to me who had a bad cold. I could also hear the scratching of Henry Steel's pencil. He was doodling furiously, as if to escape whatever further ugliness would soon surface. He had no need to improve his standing. At this early point in the school year, we all knew that he was the smartest boy in the class. George Wilkinson had been dethroned.

"Mark, please leave now. You are holding up the whole class. Leave. Now." Her voice remained even but firm. She had undoubtedly been through this before, even though we had not witnessed anything like this standoff. Mostly boys just shuffled off, temporarily chastened, when they got kicked out of class.

Then Zimmer jumped up from the table so quickly his chair flew out from under him and tumbled over, the metal legs crashing loudly on the floor. "Fine, I'll fucking leave." He stormed out, slamming the door once more. Ms. Wright excused herself and went into her office for a minute or two.

In her absence some of the boys started to hoot and laugh at "that crazy-ass Zimmer," and Harrison called him a "fucking stoner," pretending to take hits off the end of his pencil as he spoke. But the minute we heard her hand turn the doorknob, the room became silent.

"Now, where were we?" she said, and set about discussing the poem with us as if nothing had interrupted the class. For a stout and small gray-haired lady, Ms. Wright had the presence, the composure, and the nerves of a military general.

We never knew for sure whether the meeting with Ms. Wright, the Zimmers, and Mitzy had taken place, but after that day Zimmer sat in English class sullen and silent. Occasionally he fell asleep. Ms. Wright never woke him up, and she never called on him again.

9

Because my name was Mauricio, some guys thought it was funny to call me any Latino name they could think of. Harrison called me Jose Cuervo. He would sidle up to me pretty much every day, wrap his arm around me, squeeze me, and rumple my hair before saying, *"Hola, Jose Cuervo, que pasas?* Could I borrow your math *tarea? Yo tengas nada, Joseita. Me pueda ayudarseme?"* His Spanish was terrible, he insulted me, he shocked me when he grabbed and squeezed me and touched my hair, and although I fantasized about what I would say if I dared —how I would get right up in his face and tell him to do his own fucking homework and stop fucking cheating and go to hell and fuck you, you fat dick, and all of that —I said nothing. Instead I opened my backpack, took out my binder, popped open the three rings, and handed him the math problems I had struggled over for more than an hour. I didn't know what else to do, even though the St. Stephen's handbook said that letting someone else copy your homework was a form of cheating. It seemed pretty damn unfair.

When he first started calling me Jose Cuervo, I didn't know what he was referring to. Everyone else would crack up. It was Henry who told me that Jose Cuervo was a brand of tequila. I had no idea how Henry knew this, but he seemed to know everything, so it wasn't surprising. We had started to talk to each other a little at lunch. Often Henry would bring books to the lunch table—big, thick books by writers like Tolstoy and Dostoyevsky—but every so often he would look up from his reading and talk to me and Simon Park, another kid who was new to St. Stephen's and frequently sat with me.

Simon had a ninety-minute subway ride into Manhattan from a neighborhood way out in Queens. He had to leave his apartment every morning before it was light out, and it was dark again by the time he got home. His parents didn't speak English, but they were determined that their children would get the best education available in America. Simon's sister was a senior at Hallowell, and she had told him that the girls at Hallowell thought St. Stephen's boys were arrogant assholes. She couldn't have been talking about me or Simon or Henry. The three of us were kind of like old furniture at St. Stephen's, fixtures in a room that were hardly noticed—unless, of course, somebody wanted our homework or wanted to pry test information out of Henry or have fun with my name. Henry mostly ignored those guys, and they didn't really go after him, but sometimes they would say stuff to Simon, too.

We were sitting at lunch one day when Peeves and Harrison came over. They had a plate of food with them. It was all this Chinese food. The dining room was big on doing ethnic meals, and apparently October 10th was Confucius' birthday or something, so there was this big spread of Chinese food. I was polishing off my third plate of wontons when they approached our table.

"Hey, Park," Peeves called out to Simon, holding a plate of food in front of Simon's face. "Do you think there's any dog in this shit?" The plate was full of fried rice, dumplings, and egg rolls. "What do you think, Chinaman?" None of us looked at them, and Simon kind of hung his head and looked down at the table. They got right up next to him, holding the plate right under his nose. It was kind of awful, just sitting there, waiting to see what they would do or what we *wouldn't* do.

Again I started fantasizing about how I would take that whole plate of food and just smash it in their faces. Wham! Or maybe dump it right over their heads and see all that rice and those dumplings and the soy sauce running down their faces and all that. But I didn't do anything—just sat there and fumed in this silent, meek way. It was like we were suspended in time right then, like the clock had stopped and we were stuck there while those assholes tried to decide what nasty thing they should do next, and we tried to decide how lame we were or prayed like hell that the fire alarm would go off or something.

Then Henry looked up and said, "He's *Korean*, not *Chinese*, Matthew." His tone was rude, like Peeves was the stupidest person in the world. It was kind of unbelievable and totally fabulous. And right then Mr. Hawthorne came over, as though he knew something was up and these guys weren't over here offering us some dumplings. But all he said was, "Make sure you take your trays when you're done." Peeves and Harrison slithered away at that point, and I heard one of them saying, "Look, dildo, he's *Korean*, not *Chinese*," in this voice with a British accent, kind of like the guy on *Masterpiece Theater*. Then they cracked up. Henry looked at me and Simon and rolled his eyes, then went back to reading *War and Peace*.

Even though they treated us like crap, there was one thing that everyone in the class agreed on: We all hated Zimmer. As the fall wore on and the homework and tests just kept coming, I was also learning what this shared hatred required.

During a free period one day I was sitting in the student lounge, off in the corner. I was doing my Mandarin homework, or at least I had the book out and was looking at the open pages. Peeves, Harrison, and Wilkinson were sitting on this torn-up couch on the other side of the room. Zimmer's bag was over by the side of the couch. He had run in there a second earlier looking for his backpack, which at that point they had hidden under an old dirty beanbag chair. The place was furnished with all this junk that St. Stephen's families were tossing out. Kids repeatedly trashed the furniture, throwing it at each other or jumping on it. It would eventually get completely wrecked, and the school would chuck it; then some other family would haul in another broken-down couch.

Right after Zimmer ran out, Peeves started rummaging around in Zimmer's bag, pulling stuff out like he was looking for something. He was opening all the pockets, pulling shit out, throwing Zimmer's notebooks around the room. At one point he took out a pack of cigarettes, opened it up, and took a big sniff. "Jeeeeeeeeeeeeeeeesus, fucking crazy-ass Zimmer," he shouted as he threw the pack over to Wilkinson, who was now crashed out on the beanbag chair. He caught the pack, opened it, and smelled it himself. Then he smiled and tucked it into the pocket of his jacket.

Peeves was still rummaging around in the backpack and found this black case full of CDs. He started flipping through them. There had to have been at least a hundred of them in there. He was reading the names of the CDs to his friends and saying stuff about each one. They were all laughing and saying what a dick Zimmer was. Then he came to one by Britney Spears and started hooting. "Oh, shit, Zimmer has Britney Spears! What a fucking idiot. He probably whacks off to this shit." He stood up and started singing, "Oops, I did it again." He held his crotch as he pumped his hips back and forth. His friends were cracking up, and Harrison started shouting, "Oh, Britney, come fuck me, come let me lick your wet pussy!" He stuck his tongue out of his fat face and wiggled it up and down, and his friends howled with laughter.

"Oh, yeah, Harrison, my man—you and Britney, getting it onnnnnnnnnnnnnn..." Wilkinson shouted at him. Then he added, "Makes sense—Zimmer and Britney—two fucking nut jobs." He started to laugh and shake his head.

Right then the door flew open, and James Merchant came bouncing in. "Yo gentlemen!" he said as he ran over and jumped on Wilkinson, wrestling with him for a minute before giving him a high five and standing up. "Seen the latest Zimmer FaceSpace extravaganza? It's a keeper."

"Oh, shit, what's he done now?" Wilkinson said.

"Just gone after you punks once again ... he's a riot. I love his page. There's no one he won't talk trash about. For such a small little shit, he's got a huge imagination. He's got some classic lines about Ms. Wright—crazy shit and all in an acrostic poem! Anyway, boys, I'll see you later. May the Brotherhood be with you!" He bounced out of there, waving a peace sign at them.

"That fucking Zimmer! I'm going to kick his ass! We have to do something now ... " Harrison was off the couch and kicked the wall right as he said "now," leaving a black mark.

"Shut the fuck up... we'll talk about this later." Wilkinson lowered his voice as he spoke, and then nobody said anything for a minute.

I kept my eyes glued to my book. My head was now about two inches from the pages, but I couldn't stop myself from sneaking peeks at them when I was pretty sure they weren't looking. Right then I wanted to be invisible, the guy nobody ever noticed. I couldn't stop thinking about Britney and Peeves saying all that crazy shit about doing her and licking her and then what the hell was Zimmer doing on FaceSpace. Jesus Christ, I couldn't do my homework or anything. I just sat there and wished I could melt into the dirty old rug. There was no way I could leave that room right then.

Then Wilkinson grabbed the Britney Spears CD from Peeves and threw it like a frisbee right at my head. I had to look up when it hit me in the forehead and fell to the ground next to my leg. "Sorry 'bout that, Jose, but you probably like Britney too—her music and her pussy, yeah—why don't you keep the CD? Take it, man."

Wilkinson and his friends were staring at me. It was like he had read my mind. But I didn't like Britney Spears, at least not her music. Well, at least not anymore. Some time ago, I had kind of liked the music video where she wore the red shiny suit. But I didn't want to take Zimmer's shit.

I sat there hating them, feeling kind of sick and angry as hell and really horny and wishing I could take that goddamn CD and throw it back at that asshole George Wilkinson. Bash him right in the face, just like he did to me.

They kept looking at me for what seemed like forever, so I picked the CD up and slipped it into my backpack. Then I looked down at my book. My cheeks felt hot. I knew they were red. I started hoping like hell that those guys would leave, and started feeling so damn pissed that Zimmer's CD was in my backpack.

"Good boy," Wilkinson said, and the other guys laughed. We had math in a few minutes, and they started getting ready to leave. At any minute smoke was going to pour out of my ears, and my face felt like it was on fire. I just kept staring at the pages and all the Mandarin characters all over them, but I glanced up for one second. It was then that I saw Peeves put the whole CD case in his bag, even though he had mocked everything in it. Then he put Zimmer's empty backpack back under the beanbag chair. They banged their way out of there. When the door slammed behind them, I got up.

They had thrown Zimmer's stuff all over the room. I pulled the empty pack out from under the beanbag chair, took the CD out of my bag and put it in there. Then I left. I hated Zimmer, but I didn't want his Britney Spears CD.

10

My reasons for hating Zimmer were legitimate. In mid-October, Ms. Wright put me, Henry, and Zimmer together for a group project. Each group in the class was assigned a poem we had to figure out; then we had to lead a class discussion.

The three of us had a poem by Emily Dickinson, who Henry said was famous. We had some class time to work on the project, but we also had to meet outside of school. That was when I realized that Henry Steel was the richest person I knew.

When Henry suggested that we meet at his apartment

on a Sunday, I had no idea I would be visiting one of the largest, most luxurious apartments in Manhattan. I'd hung out some with Henry at school, but he had never done anything or said anything that revealed the unimaginable wealth his family had. When I went to his apartment, I discovered that Henry and I were living on different continents.

I got off the crosstown bus at 86th and Fifth and walked a couple of blocks toward the address Henry had given me: 1025 Fifth Avenue. Every building around there had a doorman, carefully dressed in a uniform complete with gold braiding on the shoulders and shiny gold buttons down the front. Most of them smiled at me, if they weren't busy helping people out of cars or hailing taxis or talking to petite women who held tiny, fluffy dogs in their arms.

While all of the buildings were big and fancy, Henry's was more so. The lobby was enormous—much larger than my family's entire apartment—and there were three men, covered in gold braids and buttons, who seemed to be in charge of different things. I told the man at the front of the lobby that I was there for Henry Steel, and he responded, "But, of course, sir."

Sir? He checked on a paper at the front desk and said, "You must be Mr. Londoño or Mr. Zimmer."

"Mr. Londoño."

"Go right on up. It's the penthouse. The elevator is at the end of the lobby."

"Thanks," I muttered as I began my walk through the

largest marble lobby I had ever seen. I could have been in a museum. The ceilings were high, and glass chandeliers hung from them; about six or seven of them filled the lobby with light. Somehow the man in the elevator knew where I was going, and he pushed the button marked PH right when I entered the wood-paneled elevator car.

"How are you today, sir?" he asked me.

I couldn't remember ever having been called "sir" before.

The elevator opened right into the apartment, where Henry and a woman I assumed was his mother were waiting for me.

"Hi," Henry said with a small wave of his hand. "This is Mrs. Carrothers. Mrs. Carrothers, this is Mauricio Londoño."

"Very nice to meet you, Mauricio. May I take your coat?" She reached out and shook my hand; I unzipped my coat, took it off, and handed it to her. "What would you like to drink?"

"Thanks. Ummm … anything is fine. Really." I began to feel more self-conscious, and once I took a look at the enormous living room just off the foyer, I began to worry that I might break something.

The apartment was spotless, and everywhere the floors shined and the richly colored Oriental carpets glowed. There was art everywhere—huge paintings and sculptures —and smack in the middle of an enormous wall, about twenty feet from where I was standing in the foyer, was what had to be a family portrait. The boy in the painting was Henry, and next to him was a beautiful girl. It had to be Elizabeth. The famous "Biz" Alexander often brought up, when he asked Henry for some "Bizness." I couldn't take my eyes off her.

The same kind of lights that they have above the paintings at the Met were shining down on the family portrait. Henry was wearing a tuxedo in it, and he was standing behind a big velvety chair where his dad was sitting. He had his hands resting on the back of the chair. He was standing tall and straight, and his face was slightly tilted up. He could have been a count or a prince or some sort of royal something. They all looked serious and formal and important. Biz was kind of shiny-looking—sparkly— all glamorous and golden. I tried to stop staring. Before seeing that apartment, I had no idea any American lived like this. Maybe Prince Charles did, or people in Monaco or wherever they were, but Henry Steel, my classmate?

"Is that your family?" I blurted out, pointing toward the painting. My voice was too loud and kind of seemed to echo and bounce around in that huge space.

They turned around, and Henry said, "Yes. That would be my family." He nodded and took a deep breath before he said, "Let's go to the library. We can work there. *Maybe* Mark will be here soon, but we should get started. Mrs. Carrothers, can you bring Mark to the library when he gets here?"

"Of course." She smiled and walked off with my coat.

I followed Henry down the hallway to the right of the foyer, and we passed by a number of closed doors before we came to a staircase.

"This is where my sister and I live. Follow me." We walked down the stairs and came to another hallway. As we walked down it, we passed a couple of rooms where the doors were open. I saw one room with a pool table and another that looked like a boy's bedroom. Before arriving at the library, we passed a room with the biggest television screen I had ever seen. In the library, there were two long oak tables, and every wall was lined with tall wooden bookcases, which were filled with books.

"Are these all *your* books?" I asked Henry.

"Some are my sister's, but she doesn't like books much. She's more the *US Weekly* type." He rolled his eyes when he said this. "She's not here, but believe me you'll know it if she comes home." After hearing Alexander go on and on about Biz, I had been hoping she would be around. Now, after seeing the painting, I was hoping like crazy she would come home soon.

Just then Mrs. Carrothers came into the library. She was carrying a tray with drinks and food on it. "Henry, where are you going to work?"

"Either table is fine," he said, and she placed the tray on the nearer wooden table. "Thanks, Mrs. Carrothers."

"Who's Mrs. Carrothers?" I asked after she'd left. Even though I had eaten lunch with Henry a number of times at school, I was realizing that I knew almost nothing about him.

"She's our housekeeper. She's been with my family for years. She took care of my mom when she was little. Her daughter was our nanny."

"Wow. So you know her whole family?"

"They live with us." That made sense given the size of the apartment. My family could have lived there too.

I didn't know what to make of this, although it sounded something like my dad's life when he was a kid. Before he left Cuba, his family was wealthy. They had maids who lived with them and all that. When they left, they'd lost everything.

"We should start. If Mark shows up, he won't be helpful, so it doesn't make sense to wait for him." Henry spoke confidently. We sat at the table where Mrs. Carrothers had placed the tray. She had brought milk, tea, and chocolate chip cookies.

We helped ourselves to cookies and drinks and were just starting to talk about the poem when we heard Zimmer. As usual, he couldn't keep his ideas in his head, and he commented on every room as he and Mrs. Carrothers walked down the hallway.

"What a TV," I heard him say. "That's a hi-def screen, isn't it? I saw that online. That thing costs bucks. Big bucks." Henry kept his head down as we overheard every word of Zimmer's loud monologue.

I was embarrassed for both Zimmer and Henry, and

I could feel my face starting to get hot. I took a sip of milk and a bite of a cookie, trying to find something to do other than look at Henry. We were sitting across the table from each other, so it was impossible to avoid his discomfort. I began tracing over the words *Emily Dickinson*, which I had written at the top of the page in my notebook. Henry pretended to be absorbed by the poem, where he had glued his eyes, and didn't look up until Zimmer and Mrs. Carrothers entered the room.

"Hey!" Zimmer shouted. Mrs. Carrothers asked whether everything was fine and then hurried away.

"What's up?" Zimmer came crashing over and held his hand up to give Henry a high five. Henry didn't respond, instead giving him a look, and Zimmer put his hand down. His clothes were as loud as his voice. At school, Zimmer found all kinds of ways to push the dress code rules, constantly showing up without a tie and with some stupid story about what had happened to it; one day he even made a tie out of some paper towels from the bathroom and a bunch of duct tape. But now, on a weekend, he had free rein to look as ridiculous as he wanted.

He had on baggy pants, of course, but today he was also wearing an enormous polo shirt that went down to his knees. He wore a Knicks jersey over it and had at least five heavy gold chains around his neck. One of them had a huge crucifix on it. I, like every person in New York City if not the United States, knew that rappers wore stuff like this. You could see all this stuff on guys in music videos and on the subway. My grandmother wore a crucifix, too, but it was small, and she went to church every day. Here was this big, gold, flashy crucifix around the neck of a small white kid. The chain hung almost down to his knees, and bobbed all over the place when he swaggered over.

He had his headphones around his neck and his sunglasses on. Ms. Wright wasn't there to insist he take them off. Everything jingled when he strutted over to us.

"Hey, food! Great. I'm starving." He reached for the cookie plate, then sat down and started to eat. He didn't take anything out of his bag—it wasn't his school backpack, but a small string pack. It didn't look like he had much in it, and it was definitely too flat to be holding the poetry book.

He had grabbed another cookie and was starting to eat it when he said, "Hey Henry, is Elizabeth around? Biz the babe?" He pushed his sunglasses up onto the top of his head and raised his eyebrows at Henry, sticking his tongue out just slightly.

Henry's face darkened, and he looked at Zimmer for a minute before he said, "She's not home. Let's work on the poem, Mark."

"Too bad." Zimmer smiled as he pulled his sunglasses back over his eyes and reached for another cookie.

Henry tried to tell him what we had been working on, but he didn't seem to pay attention. We weren't sure because we couldn't see his eyes, which were hidden behind his rhinestone-studded sunglasses.

"This is some apartment," Zimmer declared about ten minutes later, scanning the room. "That's an excellent TV—sweet! We should watch something. Where's your computer? What kind do you have?"

"Mark, let's work on the project. We don't need the computer." No matter what Henry did, Zimmer couldn't settle down. He even asked Henry how much some of the art in the apartment cost. Most of the time that Henry and I worked, Zimmer played games on his cell phone. At one point, his phone rang loudly, and he went out into the hallway, talking in a low voice.

"Yo, guys, I gotta ramble. Are we pretty done here with the poem and the fly and all this shit?" Zimmer said when he came back into the library.

"Well..." Henry paused and looked right at him. "Why do you think Dickinson combines the everyday buzzing of the fly with her death: 'I heard a fly buzz when I died.' You know, 'the fly and all this shit'?"

"Who the fuck knows!" Zimmer said, then burst out laughing. "And who the fuck cares! I'll see you dawgs later." He picked up his little bag and walked out of the library. We sat there for a couple of seconds, then Henry said, "I'll be right back."

11

"What an idiot," Henry said when he returned. He rarely said much about our classmates. He mostly stayed out of the fray—burying his head in books, rolling his eyes at some of their antics, and generally floating high above it all with his big words and ideas that wowed our teachers over and over. Today, though, he was pissed. The whole tone of the afternoon had shifted when Zimmer first showed up, but from the moment Zimmer asked about Elizabeth, it became almost hostile.

"What's the deal with that guy, Henry?" I still hadn't figured out what the story was with Zimmer. I got how obnoxious he was and how his transparent desperation led everyone to shit all over him, but he was always tearing around St. Stephen's, darting in and out of places, and always needing to use the bathroom during classes, dodging out whenever teachers would let him.

"Mauricio, there's something almost charming about your innocence. You really don't know about Zimmer?"

"No," I said sort of quietly, feeling like a fool.

"I guess that might make sense. You're new to St. Stephen's, and I imagine you don't take drugs."

"What? Of course I don't take drugs. Do you?"

"No, of course not, but practically every kid in the city does." He said this in a matter-of-fact tone of voice, like this was everyday information. Then he added, "And most of them get their drugs from Zimmer."

"How do you know that?"

"Mauricio," he said, looking at me as if I were a first grader or something. "Everyone knows."

"I didn't … I'm sure Simon doesn't either." I was feeling even more foolish now, being one of possibly two guys in our school who didn't have what Henry was making out to be common knowledge. But I wanted to know more. "Have you ever seen Zimmer selling drugs?"

"Mauricio, I told you, I don't take drugs. When would I have seen him selling drugs? I've had no occasion for that." He looked at me carefully for a minute, and it felt as though he were taking an inventory of how stupid and naïve I was. Then he added, "Look, my sister is caught up in that whole scene. I've seen her email messages. I know what goes on. She has the common sense of a flea, and her best friends are the biggest jerks in our class."

"Which jerks?"

"Yeah, it is confusing, since there are quite a few of them. Supposedly her boyfriend is George Wilkinson, but it's hard to know what that means."

"What do you mean?" I asked, a bit too quickly but I was becoming kind of desperate to find out anything I could about Elizabeth. And that asshole Wilkinson was her boyfriend? Jesus Christ—how come that never really came up with Alexander and his goings-on about his Bizness and all that?

"Let's talk about something else," he said, and his stony expression indicated that the conversation was over. I was dying to know more, and still hoping like hell that Elizabeth would come home before I had to go, but now I was also praying that Wilkinson wouldn't be with her.

All these guys seemed to know each other, and they had all kinds of shit on each other. Henry's eagerness to move away from Zimmer and his sister led us back to the poem, and we continued to work. We came up with a list of discussion questions and decided that I would make a handout for the presentation. Before I left, I asked Henry whether I should put Zimmer's name on our handout. He shrugged his shoulders and said, "Nothing we do will make him do his share. Unless we tell Ms. Wright what happened, he'll get credit. I hate group projects. They're never fair, and the teachers always put together groups that are transparent."

"What do you mean?"

"Well . . ." Henry hesitated. I knew I wasn't a good student at St. Stephen's. I never talked in class. I was getting C's on most of my English essays, and my classmates knew this. Whenever Ms. Wright handed back essays, there was a feeding frenzy with everyone asking over and over, "What did you get?" At first I thought I had to tell the other kids what I'd gotten, even though I was ashamed—I'd never gotten C's before. At the beginning of the year, one kid had even snatched my essay out of my hand, flipped to the grade at the back, then handed it back to me saying, "Good job, Jose." It was a fucking C-. Now when Ms. Wright handed anything back, I left the room as fast as I could.

"Well . . . I think Ms. Wright was trying to balance Mark with me," Henry explained. That made sense. I could see that. Henry didn't say anything more.

We went upstairs and just as I was about to leave, Biz and her friend showed up. In less than a minute my life changed.

"This is my sister Elizabeth," Henry said, "and this is her friend Kate Brown." They had on identical pink jackets, short puffy ones, and they smelled like cigarettes, perfume, and flowery shampoo. They both had long, shiny straight hair, and they carried tiny little purses. Neither was lugging around a backpack the size of mine. The big difference between them was that Kate looked like a slightly damaged copy of Elizabeth. Elizabeth's skin was flawless, as smooth as silk; Kate's had a sprinkling of white bumps on her cheeks and chin. Elizabeth's lips were full and red; Kate's were thin. Elizabeth's clothes fit her like a second skin, and I could see the round outline of her small tits, even with a puffy jacket covering them. I could also see the lumpiness of Kate's body under her pink coat. Immediately I got what Alexander was always talking about: Elizabeth was the most beautiful girl I had ever seen. She was like something out of a magazine, and it was kind of shocking—and thrilling—that she was now a real human being, standing right there, standing right next to us.

"Hi Henry!" Kate said. "Been out of the house lately?" She didn't wait for an answer, and she and Elizabeth burst out laughing. They continued laughing and shaking their heads and all their long, shiny hair as they headed down that endless hallway and disappeared. It was hard to imagine that Henry and Elizabeth were from the same family, much less that they had been in the womb together. They seemed to have nothing in common other than being tall, thin, and rich.

"That's my sister. My *twin*." Henry looked at me and raised his eyebrows. All I could think about was touching that long, shiny hair and those round little tits.

After that day, my obsession with Elizabeth filled countless days and nights. And every time I was in the Steels' apartment, something else about her would emerge—the shape of her handwriting on a notebook she left in the hallway, or the color of some shoes she'd kicked off in the television room, or some other little, seemingly insignificant thing—and I would dwell on the new detail until its place in my mind was secure and fixed. I was in love. It was intoxicating and pathetic. I became like some kind of amateur Sherlock Holmes, obsessively seeking clues about her anywhere I could find them. And I was enraged that George Wilkinson had access to her. The unfairness of this infuriated me. Yet I also developed a preoccupation with him that consumed me. What was it about stupid-ass Wilkinson that Elizabeth wanted?

Right at that moment, on that fateful Sunday in October, as I stood there in that gargantuan foyer, it was as though I had been hit with some kind of a stun gun. But despite my semi-conscious condition, regular business kept on moving, and all of a sudden there was Mrs. Carrothers with my jacket. Then the elevator arrived. Somehow she knew that I needed my jacket and the elevator, but I had no idea how.

"Thanks," I called out as I stepped into the elevator and left that shiny world, where Henry Steel and his beautiful sister Elizabeth lived, where their every need was met, often before they'd even asked. I stood in that elevator, silent, clutching my jacket. I was in a state of shock.

When the elevator arrived at the lobby, I looked down at my jacket; it had never seemed dirtier than it did at that moment, as I was walking out of that huge, beautiful marble world.

I didn't tell anybody about Elizabeth, although it wasn't as though I had anybody to tell. Every night, as I lay in bed trying to fall asleep, I thought about her and how much I longed to see her, to touch her. I would fall asleep with my fantasies raging and woke up morning after morning with my body and sheets wet and sticky. I couldn't believe that Henry lived with her, that he saw her every day, right when she woke up and right before she went to bed, and my rage at George Wilkinson increased exponentially, every time I tortured myself by imagining the two of them together.

Henry and I did a good job on the English presentation. The only problem was that Zimmer sat up front with us and tried to act as though he had crafted the questions on our handout. We had a hard time managing our classmates because every time Zimmer would disrupt what we were doing, they would laugh and hoot. Ms. Wright stood back for a few minutes, but when Zimmer tossed out that every Emily Dickinson poem could be sung to the tune of the *Gilligan's Island* theme song and then sang a few lines of our poem—"Because I could not stop for Death, He kindly stopped for me, and Gilligan, the Skipper, too"— the class went crazy. Ms. Wright then intervened and got things back on track.

After that I avoided Zimmer. Every so often, he would join in when the others called me Jose Cuervo or Juan or Tio or Tito Puente or whatever else they came up with. I seethed with rage when he or Wilkinson did it, but basically ignored the rest of the guys or just felt low-level pissed. Zimmer was the one guy I felt completely entitled to hate—the one guy who I believed was more pathetic than I was.

12

The minute I walked into the basement gym, the stench of stinky sneakers smacked me in the face. It was more than fetid feet, I realized—it was feet plus sweat plus something I couldn't name. Despite the cool, early November temperature outside, it had to have been about a hundred degrees in that gym.

"Yo, Manny!"

There was Alexander, sitting on a folding chair at the edge of several huge blue mats that covered almost the entire floor. Dozens of guys wearing leotard-like suits were bouncing around on their toes. Alexander waved me over. "Come here, man, I'll introduce you to the coach." He was wearing a huge gray hooded sweatshirt with ST. STEPHEN'S WRESTLING across the front. He hauled himself out of his rickety chair to pull me by the arm over to a rather short, squat man, who was kneeling down next to two guys wrapped around each other.

"Coach, I got a new guy for you." The coach looked up and gave Alexander a funny look, but then he stood up and extended his hand. He wasn't much taller than I was, but he weighed about a hundred pounds more than I did. He was thick and bulky everywhere, especially in his short neck. His hand was meaty and mine seemed delicate and thin, barely able to grip his when we shook. His arm muscles were huge, bulging all over the place and threatening to bust out of his shirt at any moment. But his ears were the strangest thing of all: they looked like pieces of cauliflower, all bumpy and funny-looking and kind of red and hairy, too. He was an old guy, but his muscles were enormous.

"Ever wrestled before?"

"No, uh, but Alexander says ... "

"It's the oldest sport in the world? An ancient sport with a noble, classical past? Goes back farther than the *Bible?*" He cut me off before I even knew what I was going to say. "How much do you weigh?"

"Ummm ... about 123 pounds."

"Not bad. Just a few pounds from the 119 weight class. That'll work without too much grief." He looked me up and down as if he were scrutinizing something in a store; then he reached over and squeezed my arm, like a little old lady examining a loaf of bread at the bakery. "What's your name?"

"Mauricio ... Mauricio Londoño."

"Okay, Maury Londonyee. I'm Coach Wilson. I gotta get this practice started."

Alexander lumbered back to his folding chair, and I stood there wondering what I was supposed to do. Even though I hadn't done anything yet, I was sweating. I did know that I was wearing the wrong clothes. All around me guys had on shorts, tank tops, and those stretchy leotard things. My thick sweat pants and long-sleeved shirt just added to my misery. There was no window, no ventilation in this strange, dark room. It was another St. Stephen's sauna, but one that stunk like hell.

"Everybody over here," Coach Wilson shouted as he gestured with his arms. "Hit the mats and give me twenty!" Guys all around me were immediately down on the mats doing push-ups, with everyone shouting out the number he was on. After about six push-ups, my arms felt like they were going to break. I didn't know most of the guys, but I saw two kids from my classes: Peeves and Harrison.

When everyone (except me) had yelled "twenty," the coach blew his whistle and signaled to a couple of guys to come up front. "Okay, fellows, here are this year's co-captains, James Merchant and Jordan Smith." Since that first assembly, I'd seen Merchant around the building a lot. He had this enormous body that was always splayed out all over the place—stretched across the couch in the student lounge, sprawled out in one of the hallways. Once I had seen him stretched out on one of the wooden benches in the foyer, a jacket under his head and a book over his face. Despite all the kids milling around the foyer, yelling and shouting, he had seemed to be asleep.

Today he had on one of those leotard things and was bouncing up and down, moving all over the place, pretending to shadow box and grabbing at Jordan Smith from time to time. His leotard was tiny and clung to his big, bulging body. I could not imagine wearing anything like that, much less dancing around in front of a bunch of guys in that crazy little thing.

"All right, everybody get a partner. Someone about your size." All around me guys were standing up and pairing off. Oh, shit. What the hell was I going to do? This was worse than picking teams for kickball in grade school. I looked around and there was Peeves, right next to me. He gave me a small nod, which I guessed was his invitation to be partners. I nodded back and stepped closer to him. Behind us I saw that Harrison had paired up with another kid who was also big and heavy.

"Okay, guys, you know the object of this. I want to see technique, your best skills…" Guys everywhere were dancing around, kind of batting at each other. I turned and looked over at Peeves. He was crouched over, his arms extended toward me.

I had no idea what the technique was that I was supposed to know all about. But I felt dumb, just kind of standing there, so I shuffled my feet around a bit. Then Peeves said, "Hey, Jose." I glanced up at him and right when he said "Jose," he took his right leg and kicked my legs out from under me. The next thing I knew, he was on top of me, his knees digging into my chest and his hands pushing both of my shoulders into the mat. "Pinned, dumb ass," he hissed at me.

His face was so close to mine I could smell his foul breath. The stench in the room was nothing compared to the smells I now endured, with my face pressed down on the mat and Peeves on top of me. From flat out on my back, I looked up and saw all these heads bobbing around and around. Peeves stood up, then held out his hand. I thought he was going to help me up, but right when he lifted me off the mat, he let go and I crashed back down.

Just then Merchant came over. The coach had asked him and Smith to circulate, giving the new guys pointers. He grabbed Peeves in a headlock and said, "Fucking do something skillful, pinhead. Who couldn't kick some guy's legs out from under him when he's not ready? That won't do shit for you in a match." Then he kicked Peeves' legs right out from under him and put his foot down hard on Peeves' chest. "Tough guy, eh?" Peeves lay there like a dead fish. It was brilliant, and I was starting to love this Merchant guy. "Get the fuck up and learn something." Peeves went from dead fish to standing in about a second.

"Look here, listen up," Merchant said, turning to me. "You gotta be prepared, no matter what. This guy's a dick," he said, "but this sport is about quickness, knowing how to react, thinking under pressure. Get your arms out in front of you." I threw my arms out, and Merchant grabbed them, pulled them forward, and used his hand and arm to shape my back into a curved shape. With his arms wrapped around me, I could feel the moistness of the sweat on his body and smell his body odor, which reminded me of some goats I had once fed at a petting zoo. "Okay, now move! Don't just stand there. Move. Watch out!" And with that, he lunged at me, grabbed my legs, and I was flat out on the ground again.

By my third time flat out on the mats, my back was aching, but I stood up right away.

"Okay, that's what we call 'shooting.' Don't let it happen to you again. What are your names?"

"Mauricio."

"Matthew." The name "Peeves" seemed to be just for freshman losers and Ms. Wright.

"Okay, guys. Here's the deal. You gotta work on the basics. Don't worry about pinning each other yet. That's the object, but focus on hand play for now. Just start with the arms and go for the back of the neck." As he talked, he brought his arms out in front of him and started dancing around. Then he reached out and wrapped his enormous hands around Peeves' neck. Jesus, he could've yanked Peeves' head right off. I was wishing like hell that he would, or at least kick his ass one more time, knock him flat out on those mats so hard that the sound of his body crashing down would make every head in the room turn to see what the hell had happened. Instead, he showed us how to throw a guy's balance off by yanking his neck around. At least Peeves looked stupid with his head swinging from side to side.

"Practice that and don't kill each other. Save that for a team from another school." He reached over and pinched Peeves so hard on the ass that I saw him wince. Merchant smiled at him, then danced off to help some other guys. Peeves and I proceeded to bat at each other, trying to grab each other's neck, but ended up mostly just scratching each other up. I was so close to him that I could see a small scar on his forehead where he must have gotten stitches at some point. We were both sweating before long, and we both kind of sucked at wrestling or didn't know what the hell we were doing.

Right then we were both these dumb little freshmen—but every time I looked at him, I remembered the whole thing with the Britney Spears CD, and I felt like killing him. Mostly I just clumsily bashed him around, and he did the same to me. Without his friends there, he wasn't the biggest asshole in the world. But he was still an asshole.

When I left practice at five, my back was killing me, my face was scratched up, and my neck felt like it had been dislocated. Alexander assured me that this was exactly how it should be—the hallmarks of a terrific practice. I still wasn't sure what exactly his role on the team was. He had done a lot of shouting at guys from his folding chair until the coach told him to pipe down. As we walked toward the locker room, he took a pack of M&M's from his pants pocket and gave me a handful. They were all melted and gooey and looked awful, but they tasted great.

"And, Manny…" Alexander added, popping a wad of M&M's into his mouth and crunching them loudly.

"Yeah?" I said with a sigh. What else was he going to say? That getting my ass kicked over and over was part of a huge noble past, part of an ancient Greek tradition or some such thing? Getting crushed was clearly a theme at this place.

"You gotta get some new workout clothes."

"Sure," I said as I headed into the locker room. He was right—although Alexander's advising anyone about any kind of clothing was nuts. And while my sweatpants were all wrong, they were the least of my problems. This sport was insane. What the hell was I doing?

13

Alexander promised to meet me in front of St. Stephen's around seven on Saturday night. He would "escort" me to my first wrestling team party, which Merchant was hosting at his family's apartment.

I soon found myself wondering whether Simon and I were the only guys at St. Stephen's who didn't have huge apartments with park views. Merchant lived at 84th and Central Park West, and while his foyer was small compared to the Steels', I was pretty sure that my family's apartment would fit into it with room left over. We walked into the building, and Alexander gave a high five to the doorman, then steered me over to the elevators.

"Now look here, Manny," he said as we headed up to the sixteenth floor, "tonight you are going to discover what it's all about ... the nobility, the glory, the brotherhood of wrestling. You're going to love it." He blew a huge bubble with this big wad of pink gum he had been chomping on since we met up in front of St. Stephen's.

"Yeah ... sounds good." I didn't know what to expect, and I still wasn't sure that I liked wrestling. My body was covered in bruises from practice. I was dreading the first meet, which was a few weeks away, and every time I tried to explain to my mom why I was doing this, I had little to say—a mumble or two about skill and the Greeks or something or other, which was mostly just a bad paraphrase of Alexander.

I was kind of impressed by Merchant. He was like this tiger out there, all wily and swift and strong as hell. Then there was that first day, too, when he had kicked Peeves' ass all over the mats. That was awesome, seeing Peeves down on the mat with Merchant's big foot stuck squarely in the center of his puny chest. That was an image I continued to savor. Merchant was a good guy, even to ninth graders. Most of the seniors either ignored us or actively let us know that we were useless nobodies. Merchant didn't care about any of that and basically bounced around the school being happy and jumping on guys' backs. Alexander said that Merchant was "puffing the peace pipe" all the time and that made him "rather jovial."

Now Merchant was standing in his doorway, wearing

a big cowboy hat and waving at us. "Alexander, my man," he said as he shook his hand and pounded him on the back. "And Mannnnnnnnnnnnnnnnnnnny..." He wrapped his huge arms around me, picked me up, and swung me around. I was like a floppy little doll in his arms, but soon he plopped me back on the ground. "Everyone's here. We were just waiting for you, Chief." He pointed a finger right at Alexander's chest. "You got the stuff?"

"Oh yeah..." Alexander said as he pulled a zip-lock bag out of the pocket of this Sherlock Holmes-like coat he was wearing. Merchant took it from him, opened it up, stuck his nose deep down into it, and took a huge whiff.

"Man, I love that fucking Zimmer. He's the goddamn balls." He took another huge whiff and zipped the bag shut, then gave it a big kiss and tucked it into the front of his pants. "Have you seen his latest FaceSpace entry? It's his best ever: '100 things Mitzy *won't* be doing to his wife this weekend. #1: Giving her the high hard one!' Yeah, but I'll bet that ain't happening for any of us this weekend... unless..." he said and winked at Alexander, "we can do some *Biz*ness..."

He laughed and elbowed Alexander in the side. Alexander murmured, "We shall see, my man..."

I wasn't clear on what they were talking about and didn't want to say anything, although I kind of got the chills when Merchant mentioned the Bizness. What the hell did he have to do with Bizness? We began to head down the hallway and Merchant said, "What would we do without Zimmer?"

Yeah, what would we do without Zimmer, I thought to myself. The freshman class would have nobody to shit on all day long. But Alexander said, "We'd be smoking a hell of a lot less." Merchant nodded and patted the big bulge in his pants.

"Come on," he said, beckoning us to follow him. We headed down a long hallway and past some closed doors, until we arrived at the back of the apartment. He flung open a door and inside was the whole wrestling team minus the coaches. The room was some kind of entertainment center. Guys were sitting on a bunch of leather couches and all over the floor, kind of sprawled everywhere like Merchant was most days at school. One whole wall of the room was devoted to a screen. It was a movie theater or something. On another wall was an enormous sound system.

Merchant led us into the room. I tried to pick my way over the bodies and find somewhere to sit over to the side. Meanwhile, Merchant had gone over to some junior sitting in this big leather recliner and told him to clear the hell out for Alexander, who was soon sitting in that huge chair, his feet up on the ottoman. I guessed that was how you got treated if you brought the pot, but soon I discovered that this was where Alexander needed to sit for his part in the activities that ensued.

Merchant walked up to the front of the room, Jordan Smith next to him. He started waving his arms, much like he did at assemblies, only tonight he didn't have his wooden gavel. He was telling everyone to shut up, and the room was soon silent.

"Gentlemen ... welcome to the kickoff to the wrestling season! Now, before the evening's activities can begin, I need each and every one of you to raise his right hand and swear to God, fucking swear on your great granny's grave, that anything that happens in this room stays in this room. The wrestling team has always had its own extracurricular activities—shit you ain't gonna be writing about on your college apps—but they are what make us distinct, unique ... the fucking greatest team at the St. Stephen's School for Boys!" He was shouting, and everyone in the room started to chant, "hoo, hoo, hoo ... " It got louder and louder until Merchant held his hands up again and the room went silent. I had no idea what these "activities" would be, but I was ready to join in. I sat there shouting as loudly as I could, ready to be a part of something even if it were secretive and mysterious and illegal. Nobody else seemed to care.

Then Merchant and Smith threw their right arms into the air, and we all did the same. On the count of three, we all shouted, "I fucking swear on my great granny's grave."

Somehow, from somewhere, Alexander had gotten this drum, and he was sitting up now in that huge chair with the big African drum between his legs, pounding this rhythm, and Merchant was up front kind of dancing around. Then Merchant brought out an enormous bong. "And now gentlemen ... it is time to smoke the pipe, the pipe that unites all of us in the Tribal Brotherhood of the Barbaric Yawp." He held the bong up, looked at it, and said, "and it's a big fucking one…oh yes…" Then he looked back out at us and said, "'I sound my barbaric yawp over the roofs of the world,'" and right then the whole room broke into this crazy yelping and yawping. It was clear that most of them knew the drill, but I was picking it up fast and was soon yawping and taking in this whole crazy scene, kind of loving the madness of it all.

Where in the hell were Merchant's parents? Clearly nowhere nearby, since next he pulled a lighter from his pocket, put the top of that big bong right up to his mouth, and lit the pipe. He inhaled for what seemed like a long time. Then he lifted his head up, gave us this huge, glassy-eyed smile and threw his head back and exhaled, blowing smoke almost all the way up to the ceiling. The room filled with the sweet, sticky smell of pot. Merchant held the bong up in the air and yelled out, "I sound my barbaric yaaaaaaaaaaaaaaaaaaawwwwwwwwwwwp!" Then he turned to Smith and handed him the bong.

The bong continued to circulate, and each time someone took a hit, he sounded his barbaric yawp. Every minute or so there was the sound of that bong water bubbling like mad, and then this big "Yaaaaaaaaaaaaaaaawwwwww-wwwwwwwwwwp!"

The smoke kept getting thicker and thicker in the room, and I could see the big bong getting closer to me. Then all of a sudden there it was, and some upperclassman said, "Go for it, man…" He held a lighter over the pipe part and snapped it so that its flame shot out, and there I was sucking like crazy on the top of that bong; then that thick smoke hit my throat, and I started coughing and choking, and the guy was saying, "Take it easy man, slow down, dude… try again…"

He got the lighter ready and I took a smaller toke, and the smoke came in a little slower, and I could feel it floating into my body and then into my head. I held the bong up high in the air, way up above my head, and screamed, "Yaaaaaaaaaaaawwwwwwwwwwwpp!" From across the room, from the big leather recliner, I heard Alexander say, "My man Manny, sounding his barbaric yawp… all right!" Then he gave me the thumbs-up sign, and I sat down. I felt great, just sitting there, kind of kicked back, all these guys all around me, sounding the yawp and chilling. The bong kept moving around and around the room, and the smoke kept getting thicker and thicker.

The next thing I remember was Merchant running out of the room and charging back in with a huge pile of pizza boxes. He was kind of tossing them all over the place and telling everyone to eat up, this was it, feast then famine, time to feast and all this stuff. Guys were diving all over those boxes, tearing them open and grabbing slices. Then the lights went out and the room filled with music and a movie appeared on the enormous screen. Everyone got comfy then, all kicked back on the floor and the couches with pillows and stuff.

It was *Fight Club,* and everyone was hooting and hollering and cheering. Every so often, Alexander would throw in some comment. "Freeze frame!" he would shout. Merchant would stop the film, and Alexander would get into what he called "the finer points of the director's vision." He got particularly fired up about this moment, early on, when the Brad Pitt character says, "I want you to do me a favor. I want you to hit me as *hard* as you can." Then there was this flash of an image, and I couldn't tell what it was at first, but after Alexander had Merchant replay the scene about five times, we knew the image was this huge hard dick, and Alexander just went on and on about the "brilliance" of the film and this great pairing of the fight and the sex and all this.

I wasn't sure what the movie was about, but I got excited about it and loved being there, stuffed in that fancy room with all those guys, cheering during all the fighting scenes and just kind of hanging out with that movie sound booming out of the enormous speakers and being stoned and everything. It was all kind of great.

When the lights came back on, a few guys were sleeping, but most of them were all pumped up and said all this stuff about going out to kick some ass. Merchant was still lively, bouncing all over the place, yelling at guys as they were leaving to pick up their garbage. I thought maybe Alexander was going to head out with me, but right when we were at the front door, Merchant came screeching over, gave me this big old hug, and then turned to Alexander. "Hey, Al, let's do some Bizness…"

"Might be tricky tonight, man. She had something going on with her *boyfriend*, you know..."

I was all set to head out of there, but when I heard the *B* word, my ears started to burn. Make that my whole body, actually. I started having a hell of a time trying to get my jacket zipped and did other stalling stuff, too.

"Fuck that...just make the booty call, my man. Get Kate and Biz over here. Tell them what we've got: the Zimmer special." Merchant was all smiley and excited, and it was a total buzz killer for me. I had been happy, yawping my head off, and now I was crashing back down to my pathetic little lonely reality.

Alexander turned to me and said, "Manny, you better head off without me. I gotta take care of this guy and his primal needs, you know. Be sure to walk home, man. You need to air out. And..." he paused for a moment and cocked his head "...don't be a slave to the IKEA nesting instinct!" He laughed when he said this, and it took me a minute to realize he was quoting the movie. Then he pulled out his cell phone and started to make the call, so I left.

I didn't know what the connection was between Elizabeth and Merchant, but it was clear that the party was over for me at that point. And I did need to air out, big time.

14

When I woke up on Sunday, my mouth was as dry as a desert, and I stumbled into the bathroom and drank about ten glasses of water. Then I brushed my teeth a couple of times. That made me feel a little better; at least my tongue wasn't coated with white gunk anymore. I splashed some water on my face, but I still had a kind of pasty, blotchy look. I looked horrible—but I felt a little happy. The whole Tribal Brotherhood thing had been great, at least until the end when Alexander cut me out of the Bizness. That sucked—although I kept trying to tell myself that maybe they were all just friends or something.

I had gotten home about midnight, and my parents were in their bedroom. My mom called out to me and, of course, asked whether I had a good time. I'd had a great time, the best time in months or maybe even in my life, but I just said, "Yeah…" and then kind of stumbled down the hall and into my bed. Now she would want to hear all about the party, and she would ask all about who was there and what we did and what we had to eat and all that. But there was nothing I could tell her, and what the hell was I going to do with my clothes, which all reeked of pot smoke.

Despite my efforts to air out by walking home, the smoke was like dye and seemed stuck on my clothes. Now it wasn't sweet and sticky smelling, but stale and dingy—a lot like how my body felt. My mind kept pounding away on the whole Elizabeth-Merchant thing. And even though I kept trying to say that were probably just friends, I couldn't help thinking that maybe he, too, had something going with her. Jeez, that guy was like this big friendly wild animal. I tried not to think about what he would be like with her, but images of him all over her kept popping into my mind, making me jealous and excited. Then I would go back to the "just friends" mantra.

"Mauricio, good morning," my mom said when I walked into the kitchen. She and my dad were sitting at the table, drinking coffee and reading the *New York Times* just like they did every Sunday morning. "Do you know what time it is?" I shook my head. "Noon!" she exclaimed.

"Really?" I tried to look surprised. Maybe I could get out of there fast. I needed to start my homework.

"How was the party? Did you have a good time?"

"Yeah ... it was great."

"Who was there?" my dad asked, putting down the paper.

"Oh, just the guys on the wrestling team, you know."

"What did you do?" my mom asked.

"Oh ... ate some pizza, watched a movie, you know, kind of team bonding ... that sort of thing." How could I explain anything about the Tribal Brotherhood and all that yawping and shouting and Alexander and the drum? They wouldn't get it. They weren't American, for one, but it was all kind of strange anyway. You had to be there—yeah, right in the midst of that thick smoke and shouting—to get how awesome it all was.

"What movie did you watch?"

"Oh, something with Brad Pitt. *Fight Club*, something like that."

"*Fight Club*—what's that?" my mom asked.

"Just kind of this boys' movie kind of thing," I said. My mom would not get this movie, and if she saw it, she would get all worried. I had to get the hell out of that kitchen.

"Martine, maybe it's like what some people call a 'chick flick'—but for boys?" My father smiled at my mom. To hear my dad say "chick flick" with his heavy Spanish accent was funny, and I smiled. What in the hell did my parents know about chick flicks? When they watched a movie, which was about once a year, it was some old black-and-white thing from France. They were actually kind of like Alexander, with all his "freeze frame" business, in how they would sit there and talk about tiny details and all that. Alexander was into action, though, while they would dwell on these boring scenes where nothing was going on.

"Mauricio, should Dad and I see it? Would we like it?"

Christ, that was the last thing they should do. "*Mom*, I said it was this boys' kind of thing. You *don't* need to see it." I walked over to the fridge and got out the milk. "I'm going to start my homework," I said as I poured myself a glass of milk and headed toward the hallway with it.

"Do you want help?" my dad called after me.

"Maybe later; I'll come get you." I went into my room and closed the door.

The last thing I wanted to do was start my homework. I flicked on the computer and loaded up Firefox. I had to find Zimmer's FaceSpace page. Even though I'd heard about it a while ago, I hadn't looked for it yet. Alexander once told me to Google "horny dude" and I would get to it. Sure enough. There it was with this huge picture of Mark Zimmer, all decked out in his enormous clothes and chains and those crazy-ass sunglasses. He was stretched across a goddamn Lamborghini—all laid back and cool with his arms crossed in front of his chest. It was torture to admit it, but he did kind of look cool.

All over the page were pictures of girls—super old

girls, like college girls. They were all in bikinis, with their tits kind of busting out of their tops and everything, kind of like the *Sports Illustrated* swimsuit issue. I started getting excited looking at the pictures, and I got up and locked my door. How many secrets was I going to have from my parents? In less than twenty-four hours I had accrued a bunch of them.

I couldn't find the thing Merchant had mentioned about Mitzy, but found a bunch of entries about "the fucking three stooges." Zimmer hammered Wilkinson, Harrison, and Peeves over and over. It was kind of thrilling to read about how he was going to kick their asses and how he knew the truth about all of them and their fucked-up families and all this crazy shit. He called Peeves "an abortion gone wrong" and claimed that his parents, who Zimmer said weren't married, hadn't ever wanted him.

Even though I couldn't stand Zimmer, I loved how he just said whatever he wanted to about those guys. He seemed fearless here, while every day at school he was this desperate creep, running after them, and they would hammer him every chance they got. The weirdest thing of all was that Zimmer had 276 friends, but not one of them was anybody I recognized. Not one guy from St. Stephen's, and a ton of them were girls. Unbelievable.

15

Ever since the wrestling party, I had felt better about St. Stephen's. Like I had something there, someplace where I didn't feel totally stupid—although I sucked at wrestling and mostly got my ass kicked at practice. Still, some of the guys were okay, and it was kind of a break from the daily tyranny of my classmates. I avoided the guys in my class at practice and tried to get partnered with some of the puny older guys. There were a couple of them.

I was reading Zimmer's FaceSpace page all of the time now, and it was like this weird window into St. Stephen's—or at least Zimmer's crazy version of the story. Between that and the daily drama at school, I was starting to figure out a few things about how the place worked. Our English class, which was all about discussing and trying to figure out the hidden meanings in books, was often like a chart of the class pecking order.

One day in early December, we were all out in the hallway outside of our English classroom. We had gotten out of biology early, so we were kind of standing around and waiting for Ms. Wright's senior class to end. A couple of kids were playing this game, which had started when Peeves reached over and with the flick of his fingers knocked the hat off Harrison's head. "No hats in the building," Peeves said, just as the hat sailed to the floor.

"Fuck you, man," Harrison responded, then smiled at Peeves and put the hat back on his head. I was standing about ten feet away, wondering where this was going. I had watched a number of their games, which often took place in the hallways when we were waiting for a class. They always started with a little kick, or a tousling of someone's hair, or someone grabbing a paper out of another guy's back pocket, but then grew into an all-out wrestling match or an exercise in slamming each other as hard as they could into the hallway walls.

The noise from these games often brought Ms. Wright into the hallway. She had a group of seniors in her classroom before us, and she became furious when the noise destroyed the final minutes of their class. She had already warned some kids that she had had enough of their games. During all of this I was usually standing off toward the corner of the hallway, trying to disappear into a book or the rug or anything that would distance me from the game while also letting me watch it.

It was hard to know there was a school rule about hats. There were more hats in the building than there were in my old school, where you *were* allowed to wear hats. Even though I was now more comfortable at St. Stephen's, I was still amazed at how kids ignored the rules, just did whatever they wanted to do. It was part of the deal, the daily routine, to try to get away with as much as you could.

Harrison was wearing an old, worn Yankees hat, which he pretty much wore every day. The brim had been carefully cradled until the sides curled under, and when he was wearing it forwards, the curled, narrow brim contrasted with his wide, chubby face, making him look even fatter. Often he sat in class with his hat under the desk, where he could work on bending and shaping the brim. Peeves didn't actually care about the hat rule; in fact, he broke it regularly himself. But today, that was the catalyst for the game—that and his disdain for the Yankees. That was the one thing he and I had in common.

Once Harrison had his hat back on, Peeves reached over, pretending he was going to punch him in the dick, and when Harrison put his hands down there to protect himself, Peeves reached up and knocked the hat off again. "Fuck you. No hats in the building." At that point, Wilkinson swooped the hat off the ground and threw it to Peeves, who was now leaning against the wall. Peeves caught the hat and began waving it around, and that's when Harrison dove at him, knocking him into the wall, and their bodies created a crashing sound we all knew would bring Ms. Wright out.

Sure enough—the door flew open, and she was in the hallway. Peeves and Harrison were crumpled on the floor, smashed up against the wall, and she directed her remarks at them. Wilkinson was off to the side, leaning against another wall and pretending to read a book, but he had a smirky smile on his face.

"What are you doing?" Ms. Wright was furious, and her face was red and flustered.

"He had my hat," Harrison said in a small voice, without looking up.

"Hat? Hat? Hat?" With each utterance of "hat," her voice became louder and angrier. "There are no hats in the building." She grabbed the hat out of Harrison's hand and stomped back into her classroom, slamming the door so hard that the poster of Shakespeare hanging next to the doorframe banged against the wall and crashed to the floor. I wasn't exactly sure about what happened next, but I was pretty sure that either Peeves or Harrison said, in a low, quiet voice, "Bitch."

Nobody said anything else after that, and the hallway was silent until a couple of minutes later when the seniors came crashing out of the classroom. They looked us up and down, then looked at Peeves and Harrison, who were both still on the floor. They shook their heads and sneered as they walked past.

There was an unofficial contest at St. Stephen's, among

the seniors, for who could grow his hair the longest. Apparently this had some connection with the Tribal Brotherhood and barbaric yawp, but I didn't know what it was exactly. One of the seniors, who was winning the contest, said "Idiots" under his breath, and the guy next to him, who was a close second, added "Freshmen." Then Merchant bounced out of the classroom and came over. He stood between the two seniors and draped his arms around their shoulders. The three of them stood there looking down at Peeves and Harrison.

"Oh, shit, not you again!" he said to Peeves, who looked like this little crumpled-up version of his former self. The seniors stood there for another minute or so, just looking at those two guys on the floor, then Merchant said, "Grow the fuck up."

Another minute or so passed. None of us knew what they were going to do. It was super quiet in that hallway. I started hoping like hell that maybe Merchant would give it to Peeves again, stomp on his chest or something, maybe yank his head off this time. But after a minute or two they just walked off, and I watched as the three of them and all their hair disappeared down the stairs. I could hear them laughing and saying something about kids needing to get their asses kicked or some such thing. I resented that I was a part of that category of idiot freshmen. I was sorry as anything that Merchant hadn't pounded Peeves again, and I sure as hell hoped I wasn't going to get my ass kicked later that day at wrestling practice.

16

None of us wanted to go into the classroom, but Ms. Wright was at the door, telling us to come in and find our seats. "Take out your copies of *Macbeth* and your notebooks," she instructed as she erased the board.

Ms. Wright was a tough teacher. She made enormous demands on us, and she had no patience for sloppiness or for the comparisons many guys liked to make between the characters we were studying and television programs or movies. One day, when Alexander had compared Lady Macbeth to Adriana on *The Sopranos*, she launched into a lecture about art and literature that caused Alexander, who rarely got embarrassed about anything, to turn a faint shade of pink.

She was standing up in front of the room, pointing at several lines from the play that she'd put on the board and telling us to copy them down. After a few minutes, she asked, "What does Lady Macbeth mean when she describes her husband in this way? What relationship does she establish between 'ambition' and 'illness'? You've read the whole play, so think about these lines with the entire plot in mind."

At this point in the school year, almost everybody wanted to talk during class discussions, and it was a challenge for Ms. Wright to get to everyone whose hand was raised. Today nobody was raising his hand. I think we all felt that anything we said could be used against us, or whatever that saying was.

Even I had started to talk in class every once in a while. Well, I had spoken up twice. My dad was reading the books with me, and we talked about them at home. He was more excited about my school work than I was—eager to continue working with me late into the night when I could barely keep my eyes open. But it was helping me do better. On my *Macbeth* essay, I had gotten a B-, which was a huge improvement over everything else I'd gotten that fall. Before I went to St. Stephen's, I would never have imagined I would be proud of a B-. Now, although I wasn't exactly proud of it, I was grateful it wasn't a C or a D, which is what I'd come to expect.

Ms. Wright continued to wait, and finally Henry raised his hand. "I think we talked about this. This is an early scene in the play...Lady Macbeth has just gotten news from Macbeth about the witches' prophecies. She's thinking about what Macbeth needs to do in order to become king." He paused for a moment.

Ms. Wright said, "Go on."

"She comments on his ambition. According to her, he is ambitious, but he doesn't have the 'illness' that must accompany that ambition in order for him to get what he wants—or what *she* wants."

It was great to have Henry there to explain the play to us. Ms. Wright often thought so, too; she would call on him whenever the discussion became messy, and she needed a break from straightening everything out herself.

"Thank you, Henry. That's a good summary of the lines and their basic meaning. Let's push the idea of illness further. What are the connotations of that word?"

In three minutes Henry could say more than I could ever come up with, even with the hours spent with my dad laboring over every word of an English essay. But now that Henry had spoken, Wilkinson had to speak. Having lost his position at the top of the academic hierarchy to Henry, he was forever striving to regain it. Earlier in the term, we'd all noticed that any time Henry spoke in class, Wilkinson almost immediately added something—which sometimes was merely a slightly altered version of what Henry had just said.

"Illness connotes everything from sickness to disease

to poor health," Wilkinson now said. He had undoubtedly looked the word up in the electronic dictionary on his Blackberry. That or he had text messaged his mother, who had looked the word up and sent back its definition. She apparently had nothing better to do than sit around waiting for his next text message. "So," he continued, "Shakespeare is suggesting that ambition must be accompanied by some sort of disease, right?"

"Yes, that's good. Is this true about ambition? That our desires to achieve something—maybe fame, maybe power, maybe money—have to be accompanied by a type of illness or disease, a *sickness*? What is Shakespeare telling us? What happens to Macbeth when he kills the king?"

She had specific answers she wanted, and she would extract them from us however painful that process was. Harrison raised his hand. His copy of *Macbeth* sat on the desk in front of him, and I watched Ms. Wright look at the cover of his book and take in how he had drawn Medusa-like snakes coming out of Lady Macbeth's head. He had punched holes where her eyes used to be, so she had this insane empty look about her, enhanced by the snakes. He had also put heavy, black-framed glasses on the picture of Macbeth, who now looked like he lived in a loft in Soho.

"Interesting artwork on Lady Macbeth," Ms. Wright said. "What do you want to add?" He needed her forgiveness for disrupting her senior English class. The drawings on the cover of his book already counted against him.

"George is right. Shakespeare says that ambition needs illness, sickness."

"All ambition?" She looked out at the group, inviting any of us to chime in. Nobody did. She continued to wait, looking around the room.

Once again, Henry rescued us. "No. That's not what he's saying." Henry never worried about disagreeing. "Look at the end of the play: there's a message about ambition. Macbeth is now the 'dead butcher,' and Lady Macbeth is 'his fiend-like queen.' Shakespeare reveals how unchecked ambition—ambition and its requisite 'illness'—will destroy you, just like a fatal disease will. At the end of the play, life is meaningless for him. Remember the lines about 'Life's but a walking shadow' and all of that?" He was twirling his pencil at this point.

"Yes, Henry, that's it exactly. Macbeth has become a 'butcher'; he can kill or order people to kill with no remorse, as though he were slaughtering animals for food —and do you remember how differently he reacts early in the play, right after he kills Duncan? Life is now meaningless for him. Open your books to page 182." Then she read:

Tomorrow, and tomorrow, and tomorrow
Creeps in this petty pace from day to day
To the last syllable of recorded time,
And all our yesterdays have lighted fools
The way to dusty death. Out, out, brief candle!
Life's but a walking shadow, a poor player
That struts and frets his hour upon the stage,

And then is heard no more. It is a tale
Told by an idiot, full of sound and fury,
Signifying nothing.

She paused, looked around the room at us, then said, "And that's what will happen to you if your ambition is unchecked, if your actions are cruel, if you do whatever you deem necessary—the Machiavellian 'ends justify the means' approach to life."

Then she paused again and took a slow look around the room, kind of dwelling on each kid as if she were doing some sort of cruelty inventory or something. It was pretty horrible to be trapped there, thinking about the crap that went on and having her scrutinize us.

She ended every class by calling attention to some phrase or an important idea in whatever we were reading, something she asked us to take with us and continue to consider. Today was no exception. "If you strive just to serve yourself and your desire to succeed, and if you are willing to do anything and everything in order to serve yourself, your life will *signify nothing*."

Her two final words hung in the air, and nobody moved or said anything. Then she added, "and unchecked ambition will lead to tragedy…" She looked around the room again. There was a streak of chalk dust across her sweater. Her face looked weary. Everyone was still super quiet, not even closing a notebook or sticking the book in a backpack or anything. Zimmer was sitting in his usual spot, and like most days he had his head buried in his crossed arms on the table. "You can go now," she said. We all shuffled out of there.

I hadn't figured it out then, but later on, after that first year was well over, I remembered what else Ms. Wright said about tragedy when we were reading *Macbeth*. "If this is a tragedy," she had asked, "what are we going to have at the end of the play?"

Of course, Henry had raised his hand. "Death—a bunch of dead people."

Then Ms. Wright had called on George, who did his pathetic echo thing. "A big pile of bodies, right?"

"That's right. One of the essential components of a tragedy. I'm not giving anything away by telling you this. It's inevitable."

Nobody heeded her warning.

winter

17

After four months of endless homework, tests, quizzes, sports practices, and everything else, it was finally winter break. What I was most looking forward to was the party at Henry's—Elizabeth would be there. I hadn't seen Elizabeth since the day I'd met her, but I thought about her every day, all day, and I was constantly waiting for the moments when Alexander went on about Biz and all his Bizness. He was always shooting a text message off to her, or so he claimed, and even once his phone rang during history class. Despite Mr. Hawthorne's dirty looks, Alexander ran out of class and took the call in the hallway. When he came back in he said, "So sorry about that, Mr. Hawthorne—some emergency Bizness—just couldn't wait." Tonight I wanted to look good for Elizabeth.

Before I left for the party, my mom checked me over about a thousand times. I'd asked her to help me figure out what I should wear, not realizing what this would unleash. On the one-thousandth check, when my mom poked her finger into my ear, I had had enough. "Mom, all right already. Don't poke my ears! Nobody is going to look inside them!" I made it out of there only after letting her take a picture of me.

Riding to the East Side on the crosstown bus, I looked out the window and watched Central Park fly by. Soon the trees would be dusted with snow. I loved the park when it snowed. Everything looked like it was covered in frosting, and on those days the city seemed beautiful and clean, almost fresh.

I had been to Henry's apartment a few times since our group project, and every time I went there, I discovered something I hadn't seen before. I was always hoping to bump into Elizabeth, of course, but she was never home. The last time I was there, Henry had taken me out on their rooftop deck and shown me his telescope. He laughed when he told me that many people had telescopes in New York City, but that his was one of the few used for star gazing. Mrs. Carrothers was always around, making sure we were well fed and happy. I had never met his parents—they were out as much as Elizabeth. But I would meet them tonight.

It was cold, and I wore my heavy winter coat over a blazer and a blue button-down shirt, no tie, and my gray wool pants. My mom had worked hard to ensure that the crease down the front of each pant leg was perfect. Today I had no desire to untuck my shirt or rumple up my hair—I even thought I looked good. I smelled good, too. I was wearing some of my dad's aftershave lotion, even though I hadn't shaved. It took me a while to get used to smelling like my dad. At first it was weird, like my dad was lingering around or something.

The staff in the foyer of Henry's building was fully committed to the Steels' party. There was even an extra person on that night, just to deal with the coats. Mine was the only down jacket among a bunch of furs and long black wool coats. When the man took my coat, he handed me a number, like they do at the Met, and I slid it into my pants pocket. As always, the elevator was waiting.

When the elevator opened onto the apartment, I gasped. Everywhere I looked, the rooms glowed with the light of what had to be a million candles. There were evergreen boughs entwined with gold ribbons hanging from the molding throughout the apartment, and smack in the middle of the living room was the most beautiful Christmas tree I had ever seen. Just as I was thinking about how they got the ornaments up on the top branches, Henry came up to me. I didn't see Elizabeth anywhere. I tried not to be obvious as I searched for her, while also attempting to hide my astonishment at the extravagance of the party.

"Hey! You made it. Thanks for coming! My parents want to meet you—then we can escape this part of the party."

"Okay." I was still trying to get over the glittering tree. People filled every room, and although Henry had said the party was casual, everywhere I looked there were women in big long dresses. Just like the apartment itself, many of them glittered with gold and diamonds. It was like some kind of Cinderella ball or something. What stood out most was how comfortable Henry was. He'd navigated this shiny world his whole life, and even though he would rather read Russian novels or work a Rubik's cube than go to a party, he was at home in this glamorous setting. As we made our way over to his parents, he greeted several older couples, shaking their hands, introducing me, and gliding through everything with ease.

"You must be Mauricio," the tallest woman I had ever seen said to me. She was over six feet tall, and her body was long and lean. She was glamorous and sparkly, yet she was sort of all angles and kind of reminded me of a wire coat hanger. "I'm Veronica Steel, Henry's mother. It's so nice to meet you. Thank you for coming to our party." She shook my hand firmly and held on to it while she spoke, looking right into my eyes and even putting her other hand around our clasped hands. I started to smile nervously and hoped she wouldn't mind how clammy my hand was within this hand cocoon. I was a little shrimp next to her, but it was the intensity of her gaze that was astonishing. She kind of zoomed in on me, like I was this amazing person or something. But the attention made me feel silly, like a little kid who ought to be home in bed rather than out at a fancy party with glittery giants.

Yet I could not take my eyes off her. She was wrapped in yards of gold fabric. Her hair, also the color of gold, was piled up in a big fancy twist on the back of her head. She had diamonds around her neck, in her ears and on her fingers, and she sparkled every time one of those diamonds caught the light of the candles. She was big and beautiful—kind of a bigger, older version of Elizabeth, although all sort of arranged and meticulously organized.

I finally managed to speak. "Nice to meet you, too. I've heard a lot about you." I hadn't actually heard anything about her; Henry gave me a little smile.

"Did you meet Henry's father?" Mrs. Steel turned to her right and presented me to her husband, the other Henry Steel. Actually he was Henry Steel III; there were even more of them. Henry's father was super tall also, but he wasn't just tall—he was enormous everywhere. I pictured him standing next to my father, who would look like a midget next to him. And it wasn't just height. My dad was like an old, worn-out sneaker—comfy and broken in. Henry's dad was a fancy dress shoe, polished and shiny and formal and uncomfortable. And that's kind of how I was feeling—I mean, it was like my dress shoes were too tight or all wrong or something, and yet if anyone had said I could leave, just quietly slip out of there, I wouldn't have. I was in love with Elizabeth, but it was more than that: I was also falling in love with the apartment—with this life—with the whole goddamn glamorous thing. I had always liked my apartment; it was comfy and all that, but man, did Henry's home make me realize how small it was. Tiny. A goddamn matchbox.

Both of Henry's parents exuded importance, just like the apartment. It was clear that they *had* to have a gargantuan apartment; they wouldn't fit into anything smaller. My parents and I weren't small—we were sort of average—but I could imagine the Steels whacking their heads on our doorframes if they ever happened to be in our apartment. Not that that was likely. These were people who did most things on their own turf and on their own terms. I had been thinking about inviting Henry over to my place, mainly because my mother was insisting, but now I was even more worried about what he would think of our apartment, our miniscule shoebox.

Mr. Steel also shook my hand heartily, pumping my arm up and down, and said, "Mauricio, what a pleasure. We have actually heard *a lot* about you. Henry speaks highly of you. Welcome. Have you had something to eat?" He gestured toward a buffet table that was overflowing with food; staff buzzed around the table, managing all that food. There was even a man who focused just on the roasted pig, which he was carving and serving with enthusiasm.

"Oh, thank you. I love your apartment. It's so big…"

Then I felt my face get hot. I also suddenly remembered Zimmer saying something like that, and my face started to feel like it was on fire. But the Steels smiled at me, and Henry said, "Come on. Let's get something to eat."

"Enjoy yourself!" his father said while he pumped my arm up and down again. His mother gave me another huge smile and patted me on the back, and again I felt short and silly.

Henry didn't say anything about the stupid things I had blurted out to his parents. Instead he took me over to the food and showed me where to get a plate. We piled our plates with everything that would fit, and Henry suggested we come back when we wanted dessert, which was in another room. I nodded and followed him downstairs— where I discovered that another party was taking place.

The downstairs had been transformed into a space that almost every teenager (except Henry) would love. One room had been cleared of furniture, and there was a dj playing dance music to the empty room. The pool table in the next room was in full use, and more uniformed staff people ran around all over the place, taking care of everything. There were a lot of kids in the pool room, and when I saw them, I was stunned. I couldn't believe it.

"Henry? What are they doing here?" I gestured toward where Harrison, Peeves, and Wilkinson, along with a bunch of other guys, were in the midst of a game of pool, one which involved as much swearing at each other as playing. I could see Elizabeth and Kate sitting to one side of the pool table, in a cluster of about six or seven girls who all seemed to be wearing the same dresses and shoes: tiny black dresses and unbelievably high heels that made their legs look like they were ten feet long. Sitting right in the center of this pack of girls was Alexander. He really was friends with Biz. I couldn't believe it.

Elizabeth noticed us and waved from across the room. I couldn't stop starting at her. She was more beautiful than she had been in all of my fantasies about her. She leaned over and said something to Alexander, who looked up at us and gave a little tip of the big black top hat he was wearing. He had on a tuxedo. His legs were crossed and dangling off the end of one foot was a flip-flop. Nothing about Alexander surprised me. But why were those assholes here?

"Oh, yeah, them. They're friends of my sister and her Chadwick friends, and George's family knows my family. He's always at our holiday party. He used to be nice ... before the steroids ... " I couldn't tell whether he was serious or not.

Elizabeth was friends with *all* of them? Of course I should have realized that Wilkinson would be there, given the whole goddamn boyfriend thing. Why was I so stupid?

Despite the assholes, I was kind of eager to hang out in there, try to get closer to Elizabeth. But Henry had no interest in being in the pool room, so we continued to walk down the hallway. He took me into the library, which now had small round tables set up. They were covered with white tablecloths, and there were candles everywhere here as well.

We had been sitting in there, eating, for about fifteen minutes when Elizabeth came in with Alexander. She was looking around quickly, and every second or so she would check her cell phone. She flounced over to us, clearly searching for something. It was kind of amazing to see her walk in those shoes, which made her over six feet tall. Despite his top hat, Alexander was shorter than she was.

They both pulled up chairs and sat down with us. "Well, if it isn't my man Manny and Buns of Steel. How doodley do?" Right after Alexander said this, he took a silver flask out of his jacket pocket, uncapped it, and took a big swig. Then he held it out to Henry, who shook his head no. "Manny, want some?"

"Uhhh ... no thanks."

Alexander smiled at me, put the cap back on the flask, and returned it to his pocket.

"Henry, did George come in here?" Elizabeth asked abruptly.

"George who?" he said, not looking up from his food.

"Don't be a jerk." She looked at her phone, which was now beeping. "That asshole! Fuck you," she shouted at the phone.

She handed the phone to Alexander, who looked at it and said, "Oh, Biz, what's new? Mr. Big Head always stands you up for the two stooges ... " He began laughing, then took the silver flask out again. "Here," he said, unscrewing the top and offering the flask to Elizabeth.

She took a huge swig and said, "He's a fucking idiot. Give me that." She grabbed her phone from Alexander and started to type furiously on it. She was sitting so close to me that I could smell her perfume and traces of cigarette smoke, and what I thought might be whiskey and maybe even a hint of stinky feet, which had to be coming from Alexander even though he looked freshly showered for once. I tried to swallow a piece of ham, which felt as though it were stuck in my throat. I took a sip of water and attempted not to let on that I might need the Heimlich maneuver at any moment.

Elizabeth Steel was sitting so close to me that our legs were almost touching. With a tiny shift of my foot, my pressed pant leg would have been right up next to her long, thin, silky leg. I tried to stop staring at it and that strappy, black, high-heeled shoe with its tiny little heel, which was swinging back and forth as she moved her crossed leg.

Henry and I both just sat there, Henry ignoring her and Alexander, and me paralyzed—unable to do anything but think about her and try not to choke on the ham, which was now lodged halfway down my throat.

"There, fucker," she said, as she pressed *send* on her phone. Then she looked up and smiled at us. "Hi. Sorry about that. What's your name? Manny?" She didn't remember having met me. That was like a sock in the gut, and combined with the ham that still wasn't going down, threatened some real indigestion trouble.

"Mauricio," I managed to choke out.

"Ahhh, Mauricio. Nice name. Are you another St. Stephen's asshole?"

"Elizabeth!" Henry said. "Not everyone at St. Stephen's is an asshole, just *your* friends."

"Now, now, Buns, settle down." Alexander reached over and rumpled Henry's hair.

"He's probably right," she said, turning to Alexander to pinch his cheek and push his top hat down over his eyes. He was rearranging it when her phone started to beep again, and she popped it open. Whatever she saw inspired another round of furious typing, which ended with her pressing the *send* button and slamming the phone shut. Then she turned to us and said, "Look, I want to smoke, and I don't want any more shitty text messages. Let's go out on the deck." She put her phone on the table, stood up, and headed toward the door.

"Do you want to go outside?" Henry asked me.

Of course, I did. I was dying to go outside. I would have followed Elizabeth, who hadn't even remembered me, anywhere. But I had to be cool. Remain calm. Henry knew nothing about my obsession with his sister. "Okay..." I choked out, as the ham finally made its way down my throat.

"What are you doing, Ally?" Elizabeth asked.

"Oh... I'll stay down here... catch up on some reading,"

Alexander said. "And I didn't have time to pick up my favorite Cuban cigars." He winked at me and then looked around the room, where every wall was lined with bookshelves. "Perhaps Buns will let me check out one of his first editions..."

Henry raised an eyebrow at him. I didn't know what they were talking about, although I *did* know that Cuban cigars were famous. Alexander hoisted himself up and went over to the side of the room, where he plopped down on a huge wingback chair and propped his flip-flopped feet up on the ottoman. "See you cats later," he called as we walked out of the room, and Elizabeth blew him a kiss.

18

We followed her up the back stairs and out onto the rooftop deck. It was cold outside, but the view was incredible. All around us the lights of the city glowed, and it was as if we were standing on top of the world.

"I love it out here," Elizabeth declared, sashaying over to the far rail in those crazy shoes. Her dress was tiny and she had to be freezing, but she said nothing. She took a pack of cigarettes and a lighter out of her purse and held the pack out to me, but I shook my head. Henry rolled his eyes at her.

She leaned against the railing and threw her head

back so that all her long, silky hair fluttered out into the breeze. She looked beautiful, standing there. Her dress clung tightly to her chest, and I could see her nipples right through the sheer fabric. The skirt of the dress had many layers of the same thin fabric, and the wind kept catching them and lifting them up and down. For a flash, almost all of her legs would show, but just when I thought I would die if the wind peeled her skirt up any higher, the breeze would settle and the layers of fabric would flutter down.

I was starting to think about taking up smoking when she said, "Oh, of course you don't smoke! You're one of Henry's friends. Henry who doesn't smoke or drink or hook up or anything! Brilliant Henry! Henry, quote us a line from Shakespeare or Wordsworth or, I know, a Russian novelist!" She ran over and kissed him on the cheek, then lit her cigarette. I was amazed, but Henry just sat there looking slightly amused. Then he turned to me and said, "My sister is a bit of a nut. And she thinks smoking is good for her!" Elizabeth laughed and blew smoke rings in his face. Even though they seemed to have so little in common, it was clear they had history. They were twins. They knew how to tease each other.

Watching this scene, I suddenly realized something: she was drunk. I guess what I didn't expect was that they would do all that with their parents right upstairs. But her words and her body were loose. My parents sometimes got like that when they drank a bottle of wine at dinner.

Maybe that was why she didn't feel cold, or didn't seem to mind that is was freezing out there.

"Henry, is there anything to drink up here?"

"Are you thinking of Dad's merlot or his cabernet sauvignon? What year would you prefer?" He raised an eyebrow at her, but headed over to what turned out to be a special little fridge just for wine. It seemed that they did share an interest in breaking some family rules.

It was then that I noticed there was a whole kitchen out on the deck, including a grill about the size of my family's kitchen. In a minute Henry had opened a bottle of wine like a professional and taken out two glasses. He turned to me and said, "I don't drink, Mauricio, but I don't mind if you do."

I didn't drink, either, or not really, but they didn't know that. I longed to be like Elizabeth, loose and free; I wanted to escape. Henry poured wine into both glasses, handed them to us, then said, "A toast. Happy holidays! Here's to our vacation." He smiled at us, and Elizabeth and I clinked our glasses together. I took a sip of the wine, which was fruity.

"Henry, what is this?" Elizabeth asked after she took a big sip. "I like it!"

Henry looked at the bottle. "1996 ... a very good year for cabernet in France, to be sure." Then he said he was going downstairs for a few minutes. He would check in with Mrs. Carrothers before she came looking for us. I figured Elizabeth had been caught drinking his parents' wine before. Henry would head Mrs. Carrothers off, and then we could hang out. "But," he said right before he left, looking straight at Elizabeth, "don't open another bottle, or anything else!"

"Sure thing, smarty pants, Mr. Sommelier," she said, giving him this huge smile—much like the one Mrs. Steel had given to me.

I drank my wine and felt a warmth start to spread through my body. My head was lighter, and I didn't feel as nervous and sweaty as I had when I'd arrived at the party and met Henry's parents. We were now sitting in two wrought-iron chairs, over by the railing, looking out at the city.

"Maurrrrricio." She rolled the *R* in my name, even though that wasn't how it was pronounced, and she looked right at me. "How did you get such a fancy name? It's so exotic and … *sexy*. It sounds like a … you know … it sounds like some huge, dark swarthy man with a deep voice and a powerful body and … " She looked at me again and cracked up. "Oh, just kidding!" She smiled, but I already felt like a fool. I tried to stop staring at her chest, but it was a fierce battle to pull my eyes off those hard little nipples.

I was forcing myself to look out at the view, trying not to let her know how silly and puny I felt, when she said, "Do tell me … where did you get that name?" As she said this, she took one of my hands and placed it on her right tit. "You want to touch them, Maurrrrrricio … You've been staring at them since I sat down."

Then she laughed again. But I didn't say anything. I

just sat there, holding that tit in my sweaty hand, growing harder and harder and hoping like hell that maybe I could spend the whole night there, clutching her tit.

Then she leaned in even closer and brushed one finger down the side of my face. She was so close that I could smell the wine on her breath. I looked up at her, praying like crazy that I wouldn't pass out. I kept hanging on to her tit, and kind of tried at the same time to run my pointer finger up and down over her nipple. Her face was so close to mine, and I thought about kissing her. Could I do that and still cling to her tit? My body had relaxed a little from the wine, but the thought of trying to kiss her and feel her at the same time made my heart thunder insanely inside my chest. I stared at her face, focused right on her heart-shaped lips, and imagined kissing them.

Then she moved right in on me, just swooped in with that beautiful, perfect face and kind of licked my lips. I was so shocked that I let go of her tit, and then was smacked with more disappointment than I had ever felt in my life. It was like someone had just dumped me off that deck, and I had pounded down to the cement below. Smack. Splat. But then I took a deep breath and looked over at her, a quick peek. Maybe there was some way I could maneuver my hand back onto her chest.

Before I had the new plan worked out, she said, "Do tell me…" and she kind of laughed "…where did you get that name, Maurrrrrrricio?" Right when she said my name wrong again, she ran her fingers through my hair, and I was certain that anytime anyone rolled an *R* in my presence again, I would get an enormous hard-on.

"Uhh ... my name, yeah, ummm, it came from my parents."

She burst out laughing and reached over and touched my hair. "Yes, of course it did. But why such a fancy name, such an exotic, *sexy* name—why not a name like Henry or George or Frank?"

"My parents weren't born in America," I said, feeling like the biggest dope in the world. I knew nothing about flirting with girls and could think of only dumb things to say, and it was hard to talk when I was working so hard both to peel my eyes off her tits and to figure out how to get my hands back on them. But, for God's sake, I was French and Cuban. I spoke French and Spanish. That was sexy. But at that life-changing moment, I could barely say anything in any language. My brain was frozen, like some glacier, and all that seeped out were stupid things. And the plan for grabbing her tit again just wasn't taking shape. I was kind of hopeless and helpless, and hard as well.

A second later she seemed to forget the focus of our conversation and suddenly said, "Do you like St. Stephen's?" She reached over for the wine bottle and poured more into our glasses.

"It's okay, you know, ummm ... it's school." There I went again. She and her brother joked about writers and wines, and all I could say were these stupid, obvious things. Here I was with this drunk, beautiful girl—the girl

I dreamed about every day and concocted elaborate fantasies about, fantasies that always featured me as a suave yet sensitive lover, who knew exactly what to say to make her love me all the more and want to be with me in all kinds of ways. I was also that amazing boyfriend who knew precisely how to touch her, how to stroke that long, silky hair among other things. I was out on that deck, looking out at the glittering city, drinking fancy wine, alone with Elizabeth Steel, the girl I wanted more than anything—and I couldn't think of anything to say.

I doubted I would ever be in this setting again. The gap between me in my fantasies and me up there on that deck, hard as hell, was enormous—bigger than the distance down to the ground from that penthouse. I almost started to panic. For Christ's sake, she kept saying my name was sexy, but I was terrified.

"I think the boys who go there are arrogant. They think they're smarter than girls, but that's not true! We can kick your asses in all sorts of things." When she said that, she swung her leg toward my chair and gently poked the side of my ass with the very pointy toe of her shoe.

"Oh, I believe you! I'm sure you can do lots of things better than I can." I wasn't flirting with her when I said that. I was sure it was true, but more importantly, I would have been happy to have her kick my ass or any part of my body any time she wanted to. And I would have sold my soul to get my hand back on her tit.

"Like what?" she said, smiling at me and fingering the fabric of my jacket.

"Oh, I don't know … croquet or basketball … stuff like that." Where did that come from?

"Oh, yeah, I've always wanted to be a croquet champion." She had moved her hand down from my jacket and was now stroking my hand, and I prayed she wouldn't turn it over and notice how sticky my palm was. Then she held my hand and brought it up to the side of her face, which felt like silk. She looked right at me. She stared at me, in fact. I stared back, blinked and gulped, and wondered whether this was real.

Then she took her hand off mine, which I left right on the side of her face, cradling it. I started to move my fingers, delicately, across her cheek.

"Maurrrrrrricio … " Oh Christ, she did it again, and my body did exactly what I had expected. Then the most amazing thing of all happened: she took one of her hands and placed it right on top of my pants. Then she looked at me, brought her face right up close to mine, and said, "You like me … " And then she smiled at me.

"Uh … yeah … " This was going to be the part where I told her that she was the most amazing, beautiful girl I had ever seen and all of that. But all of a sudden the door banged open and Henry was back.

The minute she heard the door, Elizabeth moved her hands and jumped up. I felt like crying. The crash from exhilaration to utter disappointment, with the wine poured on top, was like being hit by a freight train or being dropped off that goddamn deck. I looked out at the city in disbelief over what had happened, utterly crushed that it had ended so soon. Elizabeth had moved over to the railing and was looking out at the city.

"Elizabeth, your boyfriend is downstairs looking for you." Henry sat down in the empty chair next to me. "He's hanging out with Alexander, who says you must come back right away. He can't take George Wilkinson for more than five minutes." Goddamn him. Goddamn Henry and goddamn Wilkinson. "The usual drama," Henry said, then added after a moment, "and if you're not back soon, he says he'll tell George all about last weekend."

What the hell had happened last weekend? Henry might as well have ripped my heart out of my body and rubbed it up and down on a cheese grater. That's how I felt, yet there I sat doing everything I could not to let him know that falling head first off the deck would have been better than what I was experiencing at that dismal moment.

Elizabeth turned around and I couldn't bear to look at her. "Those losers. I gotta go." She started looking around frantically. "Where's my fucking phone?"

"You left it downstairs, remember? Otherwise Mr. Genius Boyfriend would be texting every second, right?"

"Oh, shit, yeah..." she ran off toward the door but right before she disappeared down the stairs, she called out, "Goodbye, Maurrrrrricio! Nice to meet you..." Then she was gone.

Henry and I sat out there for a while longer. We didn't talk much. It was kind of this weird silence thing, like we didn't have anything to say to each other, or maybe it was just that I was struck mute by the state of shock I was in. A couple of times Henry pointed out stuff in the sky. That was cool. That view was really nice, and I was growing ever more attached to the Steels' otherworldly life. But my disappointment and disbelief kind of messed it all up. The shock made me numb, and I was pretty sure that I wouldn't be myself again for a while. Shit, I didn't want to be me ever again.

When we went downstairs, everyone but Alexander was gone. A couple of the staff people were bustling around, picking up the mess. Alexander was still crashed out in the wingback chair, his hat pulled down low over his eyes. When he heard us enter the room, he pushed the hat up, stretched his arms out in front of him, yawned loudly, and called out, "Hey cats, what's shaking?"

I couldn't speak at that point. Henry said, "Hi Alexander. How are you?" Christ, nothing was shaking... nothing would ever shake for me again. That's what it felt like at that dreary moment.

"Fellows, the night is young..." Alexander was starting to stand up, looking for his flip-flops. "I'm heading downtown... some Chadwick girl is having a party... her 'rents are away, so the kiddies can play..." He winked at us. Christ, I was sure Elizabeth would be there, probably with that fucking George Wilkinson. I sure as hell hoped she wasn't going to tell him anything about the craziness on the deck. What would he do to me if he found out?

"You cats want to come with me? Buns? Manny? What do you say, fellows?" Alexander was adjusting his hat and gesturing toward the door. This was also unbelievable. Alexander was the only guy at St. Stephen's who wouldn't think twice about inviting me and Henry to some party downtown. I had to go: Elizabeth would be there.

19

It was hard to focus on the lecture Alexander was giving in the back of the cab as we sped downtown. He was going on about New York architecture or something, but my mind was hammering away at the crazy rooftop scene I had just experienced, and the two glasses of wine weren't helping me line up the details.

Had I actually touched Elizabeth Steel's tit? Had she actually licked my lips? Most unbelievable of all: had she actually put her hand on my dick and said that she knew that I liked her? Did I *like* her? I loved her—every little thing about her from her hard little nipples to the long fingers that she'd rested on my gray flannel pants, so casually, as if it were no big deal to hang out on her mega-billion-dollar deck, drinking a glass of wine, licking my lips and grabbing my dick for fun. Man, I loved her and her shiny hair and her shiny world and every single thing about her.

Henry had declined Alexander's invitation, as I was hoping he would, and I'd said something about heading to the party for a little bit, then going home. I couldn't tell what Henry thought; he just kind of mumbled, "See you around," when I thanked him for the party.

"Oh yeah," Alexander had shouted as we were heading out the front door, "give Moms and Pops my gratitude for the great gig." The man at the front door smiled and winked at Alexander. The Steels' party was still in full swing when we left, but I knew that Henry would venture back downstairs and bury himself in a book. I was so determined to look for Elizabeth, to see whether anything else might happen, that I couldn't worry about Henry. It wasn't as if Alexander hadn't invited him as well—it wasn't my fault that he didn't want to go.

Soon Alexander started yacking it up with the cab driver about Middle Eastern politics, and this gave me a chance to try to come back to earth. Right when they were in the middle of a heated discussion about some occupied territories, the cab driver pulled over to the curb, and we were getting out somewhere in the middle of Greenwich Village.

"Shalom," Alexander called to the taxi driver as he handed him some money and heaved himself out of the back seat. "He's Israeli," he said to me, shutting the door. He put his top hat back on his head, adjusting it slightly as he checked out his reflection in a store window. Then he looked at me and said, "Let's ramble. It's party time, my man Manny."

"Yeah..." I replied. We walked about half a block until we came to what looked like an old factory building. Alexander started looking up and down the short list of names next to the buzzers. "Is this where the party is?"

"Yeah... this chick's dad is some famous artist, has a bunch of stuff at MOMA. You know those artists—gotta live downtown in a loft space," he said.

"Hey, Alexander, what's the deal with Elizabeth and Merchant?" I had wanted to ask him about this ever since the night at the wrestling party, but hadn't had the nerve until now—now that everything for me had changed. Now I had to find out anything and everything I could about her.

"My man, Manny... don't you go getting into my Bizness. That's one trap you gotta avoid. Manny, you're a good guy and all that. The best, really, but Elizabeth Steel would never give you the time of day..."

I struggled not to say anything, not to blurt out everything about what had happened. I just listened to him, kind of fuming and yet frantic for any information he would give. "Isn't George her boyfriend... but you know, that night at the wrestling party?"

"Look, Manny, that's the cover story, sure, but there are all kinds of subplots, you know, all sorts of savory and salacious details and intricacies I'm not at liberty to divulge... but you gotta do your extracurriculars, oh yeah..." He smiled and winked at me, then rang the top buzzer. Someone buzzed us in and soon we were in a freight elevator heading up to the party.

"Now, Manny, all your favorite fellows are going to be here, and then some..." Alexander winked at me again, right as we landed at the top floor.

Right across from us, the door to the apartment was wide open, and there must have been a couple hundred kids in the space we entered. There were enormous paintings on every wall, but little furniture. Alexander was scanning the room, tipping his hat to people from time to time. Then he started waving at this group over in the far corner.

It was Elizabeth and her friends, including George Wilkinson and his two henchmen. Elizabeth was all wrapped around George, and just one look at them made me feel so sick I thought I might puke everywhere. It was awful. Then Alexander grabbed me by the arm and started pulling me over toward them. We wove our way through all these little clusters of kids and the closer I got, the more I could see exactly how wrapped around each other they were—his hand all up in her dress and everything, and her hands snug around his waist. It was sickening, and it was totally unfair. Earlier that night she had been with me.

"What's shaking?" Alexander called out to them when we were finally across the room and standing next to them. Elizabeth looked over at him and smiled, then went back to all the rubbing and kissing she was doing, and I stood there like a fool. It was as if she didn't even know me. Alexander started yacking it up with her friend Kate Brown, and I continued to stand there, pissed and miserable. Then he said, "Hey, Manny, come on, let's go outside."

Alexander, Kate, and I headed back through some of the kids, and Alexander steered us over toward these big glass doors that led out to a huge deck. There were even more people out there, smoking and drinking and just hanging out.

"Manny, do you know Kate?"

"Uh, I think we met before..."

"We did?" She looked at me blankly, as if she had never seen me before in her life.

"Yeah, one Sunday at the Steels' place." Now I was getting even more pissed, and I wasn't sure whether she'd truly forgotten meeting me or not.

"Yeah... right," she said in this vague way, either like she didn't remember or she didn't care.

"Look here, let's get this night going... where the hell is Zimmer?" Zimmer was the last person I wanted to see. He would undoubtedly come over and call me Jose or some other thing and be a big asshole. I was not in the mood for his crap. "I'll be right back," Alexander said. He walked away in search of Zimmer.

"What's your name?" Kate asked, although she never looked at me; she was too busy looking around, trying to see who else was at the party.

"Mauricio."

She took a cigarette out of her bag and lit it. I didn't want one, but I was pissed she didn't even bother asking. It was like she just knew that I didn't smoke, like it was obvious that I wasn't cool enough to smoke. Christ, maybe I would take up smoking.

Just then we heard Alexander. "Kate, Manny, get over here!" He was standing up on a chair, shouting to us. There were kids everywhere, and we had to push our way over to him. This whole crowd had gathered over there, and they were all trying to get closer to something. Alexander was up on that chair, right in the thick of it all. Finally we reached him. From there we could see that a bunch of guys were all huddled up, kind of blocking something in the middle of them. "Shit," Alexander said, "Don't kill him!" He pulled me up on his chair, but it was small for both of us, so I hung on to him for a minute to get a look, then tumbled down into the crowd.

Then I pushed my way farther into the crowd. I wanted to see more. Fucking Mark Zimmer was there with this group of guys—big guys, guys I had never seen before, guys who didn't go to our school. They looked mean, and they were all standing behind him, and he was all up in the face of Scott Harrison.

Fat Scott Harrison, who ran all over St. Stephen's saying shit to everyone in our class, looked like he was going to pee in his pants. Tiny little Zimmer was bobbing around, yelling shit at Harrison about how much he sucked and how he was going to kick his sorry ass and all this, and then he just reached the hell over and slapped him hard, right across his fat face. We all heard the slap, and people started shouting and saying "oooooooooooooooooooooo, " all excited. Alexander was acting like a sports commentator from up on his chair. He started calling out, "And now it's Zimmer with the right hook, one solid smack to his opponent, and Harrison looks stunned..."

I was excited, kind of thrilled and all pumped up for a moment, but then I was like, what the hell is going on? I hated Zimmer as much as I hated Harrison, maybe more. Then Zimmer turned to all those guys behind them and said, "Let's get the fuck out of here." They all turned and started to leave. Harrison was just kind of standing there, all blubbery and stupid looking. His face was super red, and there was nobody behind him or next to him or anywhere near him. Nobody. It seemed like they had all deserted him, just ran like hell out of there or something. I thought about all those times he'd gotten up in my face, calling me Jose, and asking for my homework. How scared I was then, and how scared he was right now—now that he was all by himself, without his friends. I still hated him, though.

"Oh, shit," Alexander was saying as he climbed down and came over to me. "Fucking Zimmer just bitch-slapped him … bam! Right across the old face. Bam!"

"What happened?"

"Don't know exactly, Manny, but Zimmer just let Harrison know what's what and who's who and that he's got some big-ass friends who could kick all of our asses." Alexander started to laugh, then said, "Little loud-mouthed Zimmer just kicked Harrison's fat ass. Christ, what's next?" Alexander was laughing like crazy at this point.

"Hey," I heard Kate call out to Elizabeth, Wilkinson, and Peeves, who were making their way over to us. It looked like Wilkinson was dragging Elizabeth, who was struggling to stand up. Alexander pulled the chair he'd been standing on over to them and helped her into it.

She was much more drunk than she had been out on the deck a couple of hours back. She was struggling to hold her head up, and she kept calling out, "Give me a cigarette … " until Kate went over and gave her one. It took Elizabeth about five tries with the lighter—sparks flying all over the place—to get it lit, and I wanted like hell to go over to her, to help her, to talk to her, to take her home, to put my hands all up in her dress the way her stupid boyfriend had been doing earlier. Or just grab her tit one more time, anything. But basically it was like she didn't even know me, had no idea that I was the guy she'd been with on the rooftop of her apartment a little while ago.

"We're going to fucking kill that guy...fucking yank his sorry-ass fucked-up head off, and we're going to move forward with everything, fucking everything..." Wilkinson was saying, and then I could hear Alexander saying, "Sure you are...and that's why you were right out there with your buddy tonight. You aren't going to do shit. You don't have any plan. Come on! Before the night is over, he'll have bitch-slapped all of you again on FaceSpace. Oh yeah...his page is fabulous reading..."

Alexander kept going on and on until finally Wilkinson got sick of him. "Shut the hell up, Alexander. That guy is going to pay for every last thing he's done. Just shut the fuck up." At that point, Alexander rolled his eyes and ambled away. Although I didn't want to leave Elizabeth, I was kind of standing there like a dope, not knowing what I could do. So I followed Alexander away from them.

20

Shortly after Alexander and I had headed away from the scene of the fight, or the "bitch-slapping" as Alexander kept calling it, Kate Brown came over, and she and Alexander started to get cozy. He stretched out on this chaise lounge, and soon she was squeezing onto it with him, and then they were sort of rolling around together—as much as they could given their lumpiness, the narrowness of the chair, and all that. I sat there feeling stupid and pissed. I could see Elizabeth across the room, and she was slumped over in a chair with those idiots all around her.

I had to get out of there, so I left and somehow made my way to the subway.

I was in a state of shock. I kept replaying the scene on the rooftop, and each time I thought about it, my fantasies became that much more far-fetched until finally Elizabeth and I were doing it all over the place. For the rest of winter break, I lay on my bed in my tiny bedroom and rewrote that scene until just the opening image made me hard. I became a little terrified about how I could ever go out in the world again: I could not control myself.

Then Henry called and invited me out to the Hamptons for New Year's, and I started concocting new scenarios about me and Elizabeth and everything that was going to happen as we rang in the new year together. And I remained terrified that I could not control myself.

My parents continued to ask me to invite Henry over, and ultimately said that I couldn't go to the Hamptons unless Henry came over first. My protests, focused mostly on how there was no way we could reciprocate anything with the Steels, were meaningless to them, and finally my mother looked right at me and asked, "Are you ashamed of us?" We were sitting at the kitchen table a couple of days after Henry's phone call.

"I don't know—no—it's just … these people are different," I stammered. Her face looked sad, and I felt kind of awful.

"Mauricio, they're human beings, aren't they?" my father said. "Did you know that genetically, human beings are 99.9 percent the same? And Henry's your friend. He wanted you to meet *his* parents."

"Maybe…it's just that they're *so* rich. You can't even imagine what their apartment is like; it's like a huge museum or something." The Steels seemed as similar to us as we did to our ape forefathers, yet I desperately wanted to go to the Hamptons. I was willing to do almost anything—I could not miss the opportunity to see Elizabeth.

So I reluctantly agreed that Henry could come in for tea on the 31st, when he picked me up to go to his country place. My plan was that we would slurp down some tea while his driver waited, eat a cookie or two and be out of there. But it turned out that Henry wasn't in a hurry.

"Hey," he said when I opened our door. I couldn't help wondering whether this was the first time he had been this far north in Manhattan, or whether he had ever been in an apartment building without a doorman, but he didn't say anything about either of these things. "How are you, Mauricio?" He sort of looked like an ordinary guy in jeans and sneakers. Now he would be an ordinary guy in my family's super-ordinary shoebox apartment.

"I'm good, come in." I beckoned him into the narrow hallway, because he had to step a few feet into our apartment in order for me to close the door. While I was shutting it, he was already scanning the bookshelves, which were packed into the front hallway and made the space tight and the hallway even narrower.

"Hi Henry," I heard my dad say, and I looked over

and immediately noticed that he was in his socks. "Let me turn on the light for you." He flicked on the light. Henry reached out his hand and shook my dad's. We were all kind of standing there, sort of crowded and close in that narrow hallway, those packed bookshelves looming over us.

My dad asked us to come into the living room, where my mom was standing. On the coffee table were cheeses and fruit, a teapot, and my mom's special *tartes tatin*. I watched Henry take this all in, as if he were recording every detail of this homemade scene.

"Hi Henry," my mom said, smiling at him. "How do you take your tea?" She was sitting on the couch now, placing one of the teacups on a saucer. She had gotten out the good china, which had belonged to her grandmother in France. I had been so busy fantasizing about doing it with Elizabeth that I hadn't once stopped to think about how my parents felt about Henry Steel coming over and his family's millions and all of that. Now when I saw her special china and some fancy napkins out, I kind of felt sad and also kind of happy.

Henry asked for his tea black, and my mom poured it; then he started asking my parents all about everything. They got into this big discussion about France, and we discovered that Henry had traveled around France as much or maybe even more than my mom had. In fact, he had just gotten back from France. He even spoke some French with her, and that was so great and everything. I could see that my parents were totally loving him, and he liked them, or at least that's what it seemed like as he sat there and went on and on with them about French literature and all this. Hell, they liked each other more than he and I liked each other. The three of them had more to say to each other than we did.

My real trouble was that I couldn't stick with any topic for long. No matter what they got started on—Fidel Castro or French pastries or anything—my mind would drift away, and soon there'd be crazy images of Elizabeth dancing around in it. Then I would come back down to earth, to my little living room in Morningside Heights, and try to figure out what they were talking about. But I was never quite sure, and so mostly I sat there, saying nothing; then I would eat something in order to have something, anything, to do. I must have eaten a pound of cheese before Henry said we should get going.

21

It was a little hard for me to enjoy the Steels' estate in the Hamptons because from the minute we arrived, I was looking for Elizabeth while killing myself to disguise the fact that I was doing so. It was like walking on a bed of nails, or having my skin turned inside out, or maybe even walking on a bed of nails with my skin turned inside out. That's how out of my mind I was. Every little squeak I heard made me jump. A door opening set my heart hammering, but then it would be some member of the staff who was checking on the heat or the sheets or something.

We were staying in what Henry called the Main House,

and right when we got there, Mrs. Carrothers appeared and showed us to our rooms. Nobody else seemed to be around. Henry said his parents were still in France, where they had all gone for Christmas. Henry didn't say anything about plans for New Year's Eve, and we ended up kind of sitting around, watching movies.

We were in the middle of *The Pink Panther* when Mrs. Carrothers came in. She was carrying a big tray with sodas and popcorn on it. Henry paused the movie.

"How are you doing?" she asked, as I pulled myself up from the couch I was stretched out on.

"Fine, thanks," I said.

"Look, Henry, when Elizabeth comes in, please have her come and see me. No matter what time it is."

"Sure—although I don't know whether I'll still be up," Henry said. But then he looked away from her, and I saw him roll his eyes as he pretended to be looking up at the ceiling.

"Well, if you are, please have her come and see me." She picked a couple of pillows off the floor and put them back on one of the couches. "Good night, boys."

As soon as she was out of the room, I turned to Henry and asked, "Where's Elizabeth?"

"Who knows?" Henry said. "She slipped out of here hours ago. My parents have given Mrs. Carrothers the impossible task of looking after Elizabeth. That's a laugh." He smirked.

"Was she going to a party or something?" I was working

like crazy to sound calm, like all of this was no big deal, like I was just kind of generally curious about what was going on and that I wasn't out-of-my-mind obsessed with Elizabeth Steel.

"Party? Try a *plethora* of parties. She won't be home for hours, if she comes home at all. She's not answering Mrs. Carrothers' calls. It's always the same boring story. Her escapades are quotidian at this point." Henry yawned, rolled his eyes again, and shook his head as if he were disgusted and bored by the whole thing. Then he turned the movie back on. Unfortunately, I had no idea what "quotidian" meant, but I promised myself I would look it up as soon as I found a dictionary.

I tried to get into *The Pink Panther*, but all I could do was think about Elizabeth and the parties and all the things that she and her friends were out doing while I sat in her mansion, eating popcorn and trying to watch a movie, obsessively hoping that she would come home or that something big would happen.

Midnight came and went. By then we were watching *The Return of the Pink Panther*. Henry turned to me and said, "Happy New Year, Mauricio."

"Yeah, Happy New Year," I said. A little while later the movie ended, and we went to our rooms. Even though my heart still felt as though it were lodged in my throat and my skin was kind of all prickly, I finally managed to fall asleep. It shouldn't have been difficult. After all, the guest room was some kind of big, puffy, luxurious suite with this huge bed that had about a hundred pillows all over it. I wasn't sure what to do with all of them, so I tried to sleep with the pillows all over the place. Henry was down the hall in his room. Finally, I fell asleep, buried in that bed among the pillows.

Voices woke me up. All this laughing and *shhhing*, and I shot right up in the bed: Elizabeth was here. The voices were moving down the hallway, getting fainter, and I jumped out of bed. I had to find those voices. I had to find Elizabeth.

I kind of hurtled out of the room, not stopping to get dressed or anything. I was so afraid they would turn one of the fifty thousand corners in that place, go down one of the millions of hallways, and I would never find them. Hell, who knew what I was going to find? And, of course, I had no idea what I was going to do when I did find Elizabeth. Despite the occasional *shhhing*, they weren't trying hard to be quiet, and soon I was almost on top of the voices.

Elizabeth and her friends were in the movie room, where Henry and I had been a couple of hours earlier. Crouching down outside the door, I pushed my ear right up against the crack between the door and the door frame. Almost immediately I figured out the voices: Elizabeth was in there with Wilkinson, Alexander, and Kate.

"There you go again, Biz...watch out or soon I'll be doing you, too." Alexander started to laugh. His voice was all happy and cheerful, and I could picture him taking another big slug out of his fancy flask.

"Oh, Christ, that will be the day. Give me that," Wilkinson said.

"That'll be the day … *ooooo who* … that'll be the day, *eh, hey,* when I die." Alexander was singing now and my legs were starting to cramp up, but I stayed right there, my head glued to the door, and my heart doing flips inside me.

"Alexander, you'd better stop talking about her, or I'm going to leave you high and dry," Kate said in a pouty voice.

"Ahhh, baby, you know what I like … " Then it was kind of quiet for a minute or so, and I tried not to imagine what I knew they were all doing. A minute or so later it was as though they were all coming up for air, and I heard Alexander say, "So, Georgie boy, what is the grand plan?"

"Shit, if I told you, I'd have to kill you," Wilkinson said. He started to laugh.

"Yeah, this is a need-to-know kind of operation, right? This asshole won't even tell me. Ow! Fuck you, that hurt!"

Then it got all quiet again before Wilkinson said, "Let's just say that Zimmer will be fucked, totally fucked. That asshole has had it coming for a long time. And, you're right, Alexander, the plan is *grand*—fucking fabulous."

"Then what the hell are we going to do?" Elizabeth broke in.

"What are you talking about? There will always be some stupid shit who will get you whatever you want. Especially for you..." Then it got all quiet again, and I could hear some rustling around.

"Hey, you guys want to go in the pool? Skinny dipping?" Elizabeth asked. Oh shit. I had to get out of there. I didn't wait to hear whether they were going to the pool or not, but ran back to the guest room. I was a nervous wreck, and all excited and hard and crazy and still in that insane inside-out-nail-bed skin condition, *and* I did not want to come all over those expensive sheets. I went in the bathroom and quietly and miserably took care of my lonely business, picturing Elizabeth swimming naked in some huge pool. Then I got back in bed and tried for hours to get back to sleep. I was a mess, a hopeless mess.

22

I spent the remaining few days of vacation sleeping as much as I could—that is, when I wasn't fantasizing about Elizabeth and wondering what the hell was next with Zimmer. School started up again soon enough, and the first day back we had our first wrestling match. It was against Bowman Academy. I got my ass pinned so fast that nobody even knew what to say to me.

I had forbidden my parents from coming to watch. I knew it was going to be a disaster, and I didn't want my mom to freak out when my opponent tried to tear my head off. That wasn't the problem, it turned out. He pinned me so fast, he never had to bother yanking the hell out of my neck. Right before the match, I had actually been feeling good, like maybe I would get lucky or something, like maybe I could get somewhere with this wrestling stuff, and maybe I would find some place to distinguish myself at St. Stephen's. Merchant led everyone in this crazy yawping and hollering in the locker room and told us we had to do it for the "Tribal Brotherhood" and all that. I was kind of pumped up, real enthusiastic about the brotherhood and everything.

But losing the match was nothing compared to what happened with Elizabeth. I had no idea that she and her friends would show up at the match. No idea. Had I known, *I* might not have shown up, brotherhood or not. Elizabeth and this gang of girls came prancing into that sweaty swamp wearing these tiny plaid skirts and proceeded to sit down on the side of one of the mats—right smack down on the floor and all. I saw her long before she saw me. It was like the parting of the ocean or something when those girls came in. She and her friends knew everybody, and they were waving and calling out to all these guys, but it was the way she greeted Merchant that made it clear she'd hooked up with him that night back in the fall, or maybe every night. Why the hell else would she come to watch?

Wilkinson wasn't anywhere around, but his two henchmen kept glaring over at that crazy scene with the girls. They knew something was awry, but they couldn't do shit, not to Merchant. Besides, they wouldn't have known what to do without Wilkinson there to order them around. That was kind of great—to see them helpless and angry—yet that was little consolation with what was going on between Elizabeth and Merchant, which was akin to Chinese water torture for me.

Merchant was practically naked—all of us were, but nobody else was bouncing around endlessly in front of all those girls, hugging and kissing them and joking around and all this stuff. He did this big old thing with her, picking her up and squeezing her, kissing her all over her neck and rubbing up and down on the back of that little plaid skirt. I was just watching all this and knowing deep in my being that this had to be how it felt when someone plunged a knife into your back and twisted it around and around.

All of a sudden Elizabeth's eye caught mine. "Hey, Maurrrrrrricio!" She rolled the *R* like crazy and waved and smiled at me. Merchant turned to look at me, too, and gave me this big wink, taking a little break from smooching her all over the place.

Oh Christ. I didn't want Elizabeth to see me here, wearing nothing but what I now knew was a singlet, not a leotard, and my wrestling boots. There was nothing to do but calm down and pretend like it was no big deal to be wearing nothing in this stinky-ass sauna bath, waiting for my turn to get my ass wiped all over the mats. "Hi," I called out in this flat, scared voice—exactly what you would imagine would come out of someone who has a big dagger in his back. I gave her a tiny wave.

Right then, Alexander dragged his old folding chair over next to them, set it up, and sat down—right in the middle of all those girls. They were practically sitting at his goddamn feet.

"Nice lion tamer suit!" Elizabeth shouted back to me, full force. Then she cracked up so hard that she almost started to cry; she doubled over, falling all over Merchant, who was trying to kiss her some more. And there was Kate, right next to her, who started cracking up just as hard, as if this was the funniest thing she had ever heard in her whole life.

All of Elizabeth's long, silky, honey-colored hair was hanging down all over the place, covering her gorgeous face and Merchant, too. But I just willed myself to look away and focus on nothing but the blue mats right in front of me, trying like hell to calm down. All that good feeling, that nice tiny little sense of belonging that I'd had when I left the locker room about five minutes earlier, had leaked right out of me. Now I was this even punier, more pathetic version of my former pretty pathetic self. Finally Merchant left the girls and remembered that he was the goddamn captain. He came over to where we were all sitting and tried to do the good luck barbaric yawp shit, but by that point I just wasn't in the mood.

Then it was time for my match. I walked into the center of the mats, trying not to care that everyone in that place was looking at me wearing that stupid lion tamer suit. I could hear Alexander shouting from the sidelines, "Go, Mannnnnnnnnnny! Get him, get him, kick his ... "

But then I got pinned in a matter of seconds, and the gym seemed to get super quiet, like I'd fallen down some big black hole or something. Then it felt like nobody knew what to say, or like this was some kind of funeral or something. But right when it was like a death zone in there, I discovered that fucking Zimmer had shown up just in time for my match. Right then, right when there seemed to be universal shock and mourning over what had happened to me, Zimmer opened his loud mouth and said, "He sucks!"

I walked back to where I had been sitting, slunked down onto the mats, and never once lifted my eyes from them until I was sure that Elizabeth and all those other girls had left. I was fuming for about a billion different reasons, but what lurked largest in my outrage was that goddamn Zimmer. I started hoping like hell that something would happen to him, that there really was some grand plan to dismantle him, limb by limb. I also knew that I had to get better at wrestling. One thing was clear, though: I sure as hell couldn't get any worse.

Wrestling didn't get worse, but everything else did. In less than a week we were back in the usual grind: mountains of homework, ass kicking during wrestling, and the daily Jose crap. Wrestling was actually kind of okay, even though I still sucked at it. I wanted to hate Merchant's guts, but I couldn't. He was just too damn "jovial," as Alexander put it. But then the shit hit the fan.

23

It was a Thursday morning in mid-February, the weather bleak, the shortest month feeling like some kind of endless trudge through infinite gray, frigid days. It was early in the morning and there weren't a lot of kids around yet. Henry, Simon, and I were sitting in the hallway talking about the history research paper Mr. Hawthorne had assigned when Zimmer came ripping up to us, totally smoked and just out-of-his-mind crazy, shouting and everything. He was still wearing his coat and his sunglasses, and his cheeks were red from being outside.

"What the fuck are you assholes doing?" Zimmer was

practically screaming. He was always rude to us, but this was a whole new level, even for him. He was livid, out-of-control angry. It felt like one of those moments when a deranged homeless guy comes up to you on the street, asking for money or just yelling about anything. You get freaked out and just want to get away, get out of the line of fire because you don't know what the guy might do.

I was scared, unsure what to do, wondering whether somebody—some adult or someone, anyone—would hear the racket and come help us. Henry didn't seem scared. He just looked up from his notebook and shook his head, like *there goes Zimmer again*. Then he said, "Mark, what are you talking about? What do you want? We're busy."

"You fucking tell me what the fuck *you* want, you crazy assholes, sending those emails. Are you crazy? What are you trying to do? Who the fuck do you think you are, you little shits?" Henry was kind of smiling when Zimmer said that, but I just sat there, numb. I didn't know what he was talking about, but it seemed pointless to try to talk to him. He was almost foaming at the mouth.

"You assholes are dead. Fucking dead. I will personally kill all of you, you sorry-ass sons-of-bitches."

"Mark, please, go away." Henry was pointing down the hall and shaking his head as he talked to him. "Get out of here." I was shocked, stunned that Henry could be so calm while this raving lunatic was screaming at us, threatening us, swearing he would kill us. Simon looked terrible.

"Shut the fuck up, Steel. I will personally go after

your sister like you can't imagine. I have more information about her than anything you dickwads have about me. You haven't seen shit yet. You are fucking dead!"

Now Henry seemed agitated. He was staring at Zimmer with a look of hatred on his face. "Fuck you, Mark," he said, his voice slightly raised.

"No! Fuck you! You three are dead—mark my word, assholes…" Right before he turned and walked away, Zimmer slapped Simon hard across the face. I saw tears surface in Simon's eyes. "China boy, you are a dead man, a fucking dead man, and so are you, Jose Cuervo." Then he crashed down the hall, and we sat there for a minute.

"What the hell was that about?" I asked as soon as Zimmer was out of earshot.

"Nothing. Absolutely nothing," Henry said. "It's just that idiot Mark Zimmer. He's a blowhard. A big loud-mouth coward. All talk. Don't worry about it." Henry gathered up his books and stood up as though nothing had happened. Simon and I were still sitting on the floor in the hallway, kind of stuck there, frozen in place and like we had no idea what to do.

"I'll see you guys in class," Henry said, again as though nothing had happened—as though every day Mark Zimmer came storming up to us or that his threatening to kill us was some joke or something. Then Henry walked away, just disappeared right down the hallway.

Simon and I continued to sit there, still not sure what to do next. Simon was resting his face in his hands, and I didn't want to embarrass him, so I kept looking down at the ground, right at the little piece of floor in front of me. But I said, "Maybe Henry's right—maybe it's all talk, just more of Zimmer's usual shit."

"Easy for him to say. Zimmer didn't slap him in the face." Simon didn't look up when he spoke, just kept his face down, buried in his hands.

Later that day, when we were sitting in history class, I looked across the room and caught Zimmer out of the corner of my eye. It was as though he had been sitting there for the whole period, waiting for me to glance over. He was holding his hand up to his head, his thumb and first finger cocked in imitation of a gun. He put that hand right up to his head and pretended to fire, kind of shaking his head knowingly at me. I was terrified. I stared down at my notebook, more scared than I had ever been in my life and totally unsure about what to do.

Then, just before the school day ended, right as I was zipping up my pack in front of my locker, Zimmer came up to me. He got right up close and whispered in my ear, "I will kill you if you come to school tomorrow. I will bring a gun to school and blow your fucking head off."

24

My mom, dad, and I sat in Mitzy's office the next morning for about ten minutes before he arrived. His assistant told us Mitzy was teaching his first period class, but should be back shortly.

I'd gone home the night before and agonized for a couple of hours, but finally became so petrified that I told my parents what had happened. After hours of worry, I'd finally decided that being a narc wasn't worse than being murdered. It was pretty bad, but death had to be worse. The minute I told my parents, they called Mitzy, and here we were.

The office was cramped with furniture and stacks of

papers everywhere, and we sat on three chairs around a small round table. I sat between my parents, and my mom held my hand. Normally I would have refused to let her do this. Today, it was okay. Today I longed for the days when my mother held my hand everywhere we went, back when we would go to Central Park and the Natural History Museum. I was maybe three or four then. Now my mother kept looking at me and squeezing my hand. We all felt nervous and awkward.

"Mauricio, what was the boy's name again?"

"Mark Zimmer."

"Why would he threaten you like that?"

"I don't know, Mama. Guys don't like him. He's hard to like," I said quietly. "I told you about him. He was in that group project with me and Henry."

"Do you think he knew you were angry about the project?"

"Dad, he didn't know. Henry and I didn't say anything. We didn't even tell our teacher what happened."

Just then Mitzy burst into the office, and we all stood up. My father held out his hand, "Carlos Londoño. We met at the new parents' reception a few months ago."

"Yes, of course, Mr. Londoño. Thank you for calling me and for coming in today." He shook my mom's hand and asked us to sit down.

Mitzy looked exhausted. My father had called him about ten o'clock the night before, and Mitzy looked like he'd been up for hours after that. There were dark circles under his eyes, his clothes were rumpled, and when he moved, his body looked tired and achy, as if doing everyday things like walking or crossing his legs was painful. I started to wonder whether he had come back to school after my dad called him. Maybe he had just stayed in his office all night working, trying to figure out what to do.

"I'm sorry that we have to meet under these conditions. We're doing everything we can to figure out what happened. This kind of behavior is unacceptable at St. Stephen's." Mitzy stopped speaking for a moment, then looked right at me. "Mauricio, there were three email messages sent from your St. Stephen's account to Mark Zimmer. Messages that threatened him and accused him of doing terrible things— illegal things." He paused for a moment, then continued. "The messages were all sent late on Wednesday night . . . actually, it would have been early Thursday morning. Do you know anything about the messages? Have you ever emailed Mark Zimmer?" He looked right at me and waited for me to speak. My mother squeezed my hand.

"Mr. Mitz, I don't know anything. I didn't send them." My voice was shaky and soft.

"Have you ever sent any messages to Mark? About anything?" He continued to look right at me, to stare at me, and I started to feel even more uncomfortable under this close watch—like maybe this guy didn't believe me.

"I *didn't* send those messages. I wasn't even awake then. I may have emailed him once. Well, Henry did, and I was on the email, too, about our English project."

"What English project? When was that?" Mitzy had grabbed a yellow pad and was writing something down.

"It was this group project—months ago—on Emily Dickinson. A poem of hers, you know … about a fly … "

"Who was in the group?"

"Me, Henry, and Zim … Mark, I mean."

"Why were you sending email? Or why was Henry sending email?"

"We were figuring out when we would meet. We had to meet on a Sunday to do the work." Whenever I said anything, Mitzy would write stuff down. My mom was still holding my hand; in fact, by this point she was squeezing my hand hard.

"Where were you meeting?" Mitzy asked.

"At Henry's place—over on the East Side."

"Mauricio didn't send those messages! He wouldn't do anything like this," my mother broke in. Although both of my parents had been sitting there quietly, she couldn't take it anymore. "Mauricio would never do anything like this," she said again. "He didn't even know about all of this email mailings and FaceSpace World Wide Web before he came to this school!"

My mother didn't *really* know what I did or didn't know, but she was right that there had been far less of this stuff in my life before St. Stephen's. My old school had very few computers, and the ones they did have were old and slow. Only one computer in the school had Internet access, and it was impossible to use it. St. Stephen's had hundreds of brand-new computers in five computer labs.

"Mrs. Londoño, I understand your concern. If this were my son, I would feel the same way. We all want to protect our children as much as we can. That's what we have to do as parents, and my job is to take care of all of the children at St. Stephen's."

"Is it possible that someone else—someone outside of St. Stephen's—got into this Internet business and used these email letters?" My dad didn't know much about computers either. He had to use email for work, but he had a research assistant who printed out his messages and helped him with sending them.

"It's not impossible, no, and believe me, we have considered the possibility. We are fairly certain they were written by someone in the community, but we will be able to know for sure once we trace the computer or computers used. We can do that, and we're going to." He looked at us, waiting for a response. When none of us said anything, he continued. "Mauricio, do you think someone has your login and password information? Did you ever give it to anyone?"

"No ... never," I said. But obviously some *assholes* in my class got my information, I thought. "I'm the only one who has it. It's possible someone watched me log in. I try to be careful, but it's crowded in the computer labs."

I was hoping he was almost through with us. I wanted to leave.

Mitzy put down his notepad, then shuffled a few papers

around on his desk, glancing at them quickly. "You do know that there are ways to trace emails, back to the computer from which they were sent. We're in the process of doing that. If someone else used your account to send the messages, we'll be able to find the computer that person used, whether it's a school computer or not." He was looking from my mom to my dad and then to me. He was pretty calm the whole time, and I couldn't tell what he was suggesting. Was he getting at how they would find out who did this to me? Who used my account to send the messages? Or was he telling me that I should confess? Maybe he really thought I did this? Didn't Mitzy know that I was just some dumb-shit, stupid-ass Jose Cuervo? I felt sick and wanted to get out of that cramped office.

"Mr. Mitzenmacher," my father said, "what did the messages say?"

"Of course, you would want to know this; of course you do, but I've been advised by the school lawyer to keep the content confidential. What I can tell you is that their content accused Mark Zimmer of being involved in illegal activities, and there were threats along with several incriminating photos."

Now I was fuming. It felt like my head was going to blow off. Those assholes who had threatened to get Zimmer, who had concocted some big "grand plan," had used my email account to send him messages, to threaten him—and they made it look like I was the one going after him. I sat there stunned. Mitzy kept right on talking in this calm, steady voice. I started to hate him, too.

"Mr. Mitzenmacher," my dad said, "how do we know our son will be safe here at St. Stephen's? That boy—that Mark Zimmer—told Mauricio he would kill him. He said he had a gun…"

"Mark Zimmer is no longer at St. Stephen's. We have taken his threats very seriously." Just like that, Zimmer was gone.

Mitzy sat there for another minute or two, kind of holding his hands together like he didn't know what to do with them. No one knew what to say, but I could tell my parents weren't done yet. Finally Mitzy said, "Mauricio, if you think of anything else or anything you want to talk about, please come and talk with me. Anything you tell me is confidential." Bullshit, I thought. Nothing in this place is confidential, and soon every guy in the school would know that Mark Zimmer had scared the shit out of me. "Mr. and Mrs. Londoño, I'm sorry you had to come in for this. Truly. Please know how pleased everyone at St. Stephen's is that Mauricio is here with us. He's a very fine addition to the community. He's a very fine young man. I'm sure you are proud of him."

"But, Mr. Mitzenmacher," my father broke in, even though it was clear that Mitzy was trying as hard as I was to get out of there, "what kind of school is this where boys do these things to each other? What is going on here?" I knew that was coming. My parents had argued about St. Stephen's the night before, and my dad kept coming back to how he couldn't believe all this stuff was going on in this elite place, how the adults had to be as much the problem as any kids.

"Mr. Londoño, Mrs. Londoño—" Mitzy looked at each of my parents. "Let me assure you that we will do everything we can to find out what is going on. This event is most unusual for the school." He paused for a moment or two and kind of wrung his hands together while taking a deep breath. Then he continued. "I have dedicated my professional life to educating boys to become fine young men, men who will make meaningful contributions to society. Please know that that is our sincere intention ... and please know that keeping children safe is more important than anything else—" His voice broke off, and my parents sat there, baffled and unsure whom to believe. By then Mitzy looked even more exhausted than he had when he'd first come into the office—now it was as though just shaping words and forming sentences were painful.

Then we all stood up. Mitzy reached out and shook my hand first and then each of my parents'. We said goodbye, and I walked my parents down to the lobby. We didn't say anything as we walked. In the lobby both of them hugged and kissed me. Today I let them. I didn't care who saw us. Then I hurried to class. I was late, and I just wanted to sit in biology and think about photosynthesis or chromosomes or sickle cell anemia or anything. Despite what Mitzy had said about Zimmer, all day I kept worrying that I would run into him. But I never did. He was gone from St. Stephen's—and, in fact, I never saw him again.

25

It was soon clear that the entire freshman class was on every upperclassman's shit list, and every one of them who walked by us had an insult or a snide remark to make. Mitzy had closed all the computer labs, and the upperclassmen were enraged and took every chance they got to let us know what they thought.

Jordan Smith, co-captain of the wrestling team, walked up to a group of us when we were standing in the hallway, waiting to go in to geometry. "You bunch of fucking morons," he said. He got so close to a couple of freshmen leaning against the wall that it seemed like he was going to hit them. But then he walked off, continuing to curse us. Once again I was walking around the school feeling kind of scared—although it was different this time. I was nervous, but I was also furious. I hadn't done anything, and I didn't know anything.

Rumors were flying all over the school about the emails and Zimmer's disappearance. I was relieved that he wasn't around, although I was still watching my back everywhere I went, especially when I left school. I kept imagining Zimmer showing up with the guys who had been with him at that party. Maybe he would go after *me* now, just like he had Harrison that night, all up in his face and slapping him around. Or maybe he would do what he said he would do. How the hell did I know what Zimmer was capable of?

Henry tried to assure me over and over that there was nothing to worry about. But what the hell did *he* have to worry about? He took two steps out of the school building and was shuttled off in his private car. It wasn't like he was standing around on the subway platform or at the bus stop, an easy target for a lunatic with a gun.

Simon hadn't been to school since the day that Zimmer screamed at us, but it wasn't until the following week that we learned he wasn't coming back at all. He had transferred to Stuyvesant.

That same week, on Wednesday morning, I arrived at St. Stephen's and saw a big sign on the front door announcing a freshman class meeting, in Room 315, during first period. This had to be some huge deal, because I had a biology test first period.

Walking to Room 315, I passed one of the computer labs and noticed that it was open. I could hear some of the upperclassmen inside, complaining loudly. "What is this, fucking North Korea? No Internet access! This school sucks. Mitzy sucks. That asshole." Kids could use the computers again, it seemed, but the wireless network and the Internet had been shut down.

Inside Room 315, sitting up front, were the headmaster of St. Stephens, Mr. Hutchinson; the computer teacher, Harky; and a man I had never seen before. Mitzy was at the door, ushering kids in and getting them to sit down. By 8:30 the room was packed. The desks and chairs had been stacked in the hallway, and every inch of floor space was filled with the seventy-five members of my class.

Mitzy shut the door and walked to the front of the room. It was already like a sauna, and I wondered why nobody ever thought about opening the windows in this school.

"We are in the midst of a crisis, and we are taking time from one of your classes because we have critical information to share with all of you. Some of you are even missing your test." Mitzy stopped talking for a minute and turned to the man I had never seen before, who was sitting at the table.

"I want to introduce Detective Finnegan of the NYPD. We contacted him last Friday to help us with the investigation, and to help us understand what the criminal issues are. Mr. Harker will then explain some of the technical aspects of what happened."

Detective Finnegan stood up, and Mitzy walked over to the table and sat down. Detective Finnegan was wearing a suit and tie. His hair was red and thinning, and he was chewing gum. "Now, listen up, boys. There are criminal issues here. I guarantee you that we will find the guys who did this. It would be much easier if you just turn yourselves in. It would be easier for you and your families. Mr. Harker will tell you more about all the ins and outs of what happened, but I'm here to tell you that there are serious matters here."

Jesus Christ. What did those guys do? What had been their "grand plan"? I could feel my heart start to beat harder. I kept my eyes on the carpet and tried to control my breath, slow my heart down. I was desperate to look up. I wanted to see the faces of my classmates. I wanted to see the panic that I assumed would be on some of them. But I willed myself to keep my eyes on that gray carpet. I bore my eyes into it, focusing all my energy on not moving my head and listening to the detective, waiting to find out what horrible things those guys had done.

Then my mind flipped to Elizabeth, as it did about a gazillion times a day, and that completely messed up my efforts to slow my heart down. I kept trying to calm down, but I was getting really excited thinking about how she might break up with Wilkinson. Maybe she would finally get what a shithead he was.

Then Harky stood up. "What we've pieced together is

the following: somebody installed a keystroke recorder on one of the computers in the first-floor computer lab, the one many of you use every day. As the name suggests, a keystroke recorder can record every key that someone types on a particular computer."

Christ. Whoever did this had been able to read everything typed on that computer. Everything. Every email, instant message, every web address, everything.

"With a keystroke recorder, you can read what's been typed, including, of course, login and password information. That's how someone obtained other people's login and password information. We don't know when the keystroke recorder was installed—it could have been on the computer for months, maybe longer—so it's possible that whoever did this has the login and password information of more than just three students."

Mitzy stood up then and said, "Because of that, we have shut down the wireless network and the Internet altogether, and we're in the process of changing our system. And boys, let me tell you—that's not cheap."

"That's right," Harky said. He spoke in a monotone, delivering the information as if he were simply reading announcements in the daily bulletin. "And our server has a record of everything that is sent out from every computer in the school, whether through email or instant message. We're now looking at all of this." He paused and looked out at all of us. "You should not be doing things on our computers, or any computer, that you wouldn't want Mr. Mitz or your mother or father to read." Now he was shaking his head in this totally disgusted way. "This is one hell of a job, but we've already retrieved the emails that were sent to Mark Zimmer."

I could feel discomfort spreading through the room. Every boy in that room had done something on the school's computers that he wouldn't want Mitzy, and certainly not his parents, to know about. That cold creepy feeling—the feeling of fear and panic that spreads through your body when you get caught doing something wrong—was now seeping through that packed room. I tried to remember whether there was much I'd done. I'd spent a lot of time looking at the Chadwick website, trying to find pictures of Elizabeth and just kind of enjoying prowling around those images—all those happy, smiling girls in those little plaid skirts.

Harky wasn't finished yet. "Now that we know about the keystroke recorder and how the three accounts were accessed, we're moving forward with determining which computers actually sent the emails."

Detective Finnegan spoke up at this point. "We aren't ruling out the possibility that someone broke into the school. That's possible. It's also possible that someone broke in just to install the keystroke recorder. If that's the case, we may have other crimes to deal with—like breaking and entering."

Harky continued. "Every computer in the world has an IP address, which is like a social security number. Every computer has a unique one. That's how we can figure out which computers sent the emails, whether they're school computers or not. That's what we're working on now, and I expect we will figure this out today or tomorrow." He still spoke in the most matter-of-fact manner, as if he were ordering breakfast in a diner or asking the cleaners for no starch and a box for his shirts.

I knew that a part of Harky had to be secretly pleased, maybe even overjoyed. He spent so much time telling kids not to play games or to get off certain websites. He had to be sick of patrolling the computer labs. But Christ, his voice was annoying.

Detective Finnegan looked ready to move on. "This is a pretty routine investigation," he said.

At this point, Henry raised his hand. "Detective, I'm one of the students whose accounts were used to send the messages. I'm wondering whether there are charges that I personally can bring against whoever did this."

I had no idea what Henry was doing. He was going to press charges himself? Maybe go after Zimmer, too?

The detective looked over at Mitzy, who nodded at him. "Yes, there are charges you can file. You contact my precinct if you want to move forward. For now, just let me and Mr. Mitzenmacher work on this. When we find out who did this, that person or persons will be sorry. I can promise you that."

I was starting to feel a mixture of excitement and anxiety. They were going to discover who did this. What could those guys do now? Throw away their computers? They were going to get caught. It was weird, though. Kind of creepy. Knowing the school could get all this information about us. Knowing they could see anything we did on the computers. Those guys couldn't have imagined what would end up happening. The police were involved. Maybe they would go to jail.

Mitzy stood up and thanked the detective for his help. He asked us whether anyone else had questions, but not one hand went up. The room was silent except for the occasional clanging from the radiator, which just kept on spitting out heat. It was stifling in there.

26

B oys," Mitzy said, "there are a few other things you need to know. Mr. Hutchinson will cover these matters."

What now, I thought. What else could we possibly be hit with? Yet it turned out that there were more than a few matters to cover. There were actually about a billion things awry at the St. Stephen's School for Boys.

Mr. Hutchinson stood up, and there wasn't a trace of joy in his face. Our jolly headmaster now looked like a shadowy version of his former self, his sagging face contrasting sharply with the brightness of his starched white shirt.

"Boys, this is a serious situation." He paused and looked around the room. I was still trying to melt into the rug.

Although Mr. Hutchinson wasn't nearly as tall as Mitzy, he was thick and hearty looking. At the beginning of the year, he'd given a talk to the high school. I remembered that he said he could never get into St. Stephen's now, or Princeton either, where he had gone to college. He joked that he was "old school" in the true sense of the phrase. He told us about the "Gentleman's C"—but his point was that all of this was gone. Prep schools had become fiercely competitive, particularly in New York City where there weren't enough spots for all the qualified kids. He wanted us to know that being admitted to St. Stephen's was a big accomplishment, and that we had a responsibility to take advantage of what the school offered.

"We're learning a lot right now about technology," Hutchinson began. "And, in particular, we're learning about how St. Stephen's students are using it. Perhaps we should have done a better job of staying informed about all these new developments." He paused. "That said, it doesn't excuse what students have done here at the school. What you also must know is that we have learned a lot about what some of you seem to be doing with drugs and alcohol. There may be some very dangerous things going on." He looked at us for a few moments. "We've been naïve, and it's painful to discover all of this. It's also terrifying, and we have to do everything we can to ensure your safety." His voice was stern and severe, and underneath there was sadness. He paused again for what seemed like the longest minute ever.

"In order to keep you safe, we are imposing several new rules. We now know that some of you are abusing your cell phone and graphing-calculator privileges. Apparently there are students who, despite having signed the St. Stephen's Code of Honor and Ethics, store information about tests on their graphing calculators. They pass that information on to students who are taking the test later in the day." He looked around the room. "Similar things go on with cell phones. There are students who take pictures of tests with their cell phones and pass the pictures on to other students. These are egregious instances of cheating. Students will no longer be allowed to use either cell phones or graphing calculators at St. Stephen's. Don't bring them to school." All over the room protests broke out, and students began to raise their hands.

Harky chimed in. "And that means no Palm Pilots, BlackBerries, Sidekicks, or any other electronic device." The talking among the students started to intensify.

"Silence," Mr. Hutchinson bellowed. I had never heard him speak so angrily before. His face had turned bright red, and he wiped his forehead with a handkerchief. The room became silent, although a few boys kept their hands in the air. All the noise had to come from anxiety. Nobody knew what they did or didn't know about drugs and alcohol and what went on. Even I started worrying about whether they had found out about the wrestling parties and the barbaric bong hits and all that.

"Boys, some of the information we have suggests that there is illegal drug activity taking place both at school and after school. From now on, nobody will be allowed to leave the buildings during the school day, and we are considering random drug testing. This is not the St. Stephen's way, but we may have no choice."

Right then Mitzy stood up, eager to end the meeting and unleash us on our second period teachers. "Boys, I am sure you have often heard adults tell you that something you don't like is for your own good. We have a situation that is out of control, and we must rein it in." As he looked around the room, almost every boy in there looked back at him with hatred in his eyes.

"If you know anything about what happened, come forward. Do the right thing." He waited a few moments, then said, "Second period has already started—go to your classes. Quickly."

The room broke into activity as everyone gathered up his stuff and headed toward the door. Everybody was eager to complain about the new rules, but beneath all the protests was fear. What did they know? And what the hell was the "right thing" to do?

Later that day, I learned from Alexander—who had somehow made it to the meeting—that they had Zimmer's computer. Actually, the police had it. Alexander had dropped in on Mitzy during lunch and had a "chitty chat" with him about the "issues," as Alexander called them. He also knew that Mitzy and Hutch knew about the graphing calculator and cell phone stuff from teachers—apparently there had been a faculty meeting where the teachers went nuts about the cheating at the school.

"But, that's not the thing," Alexander said. "What they've really got to do, what they've got to clean up as quickly as possible, is all this business with the St. Stephen's gentlemen and drugs. Imagine the headlines in the *New York Post*." He shook his head and cracked up laughing.

27

Harky and Detective Finnegan were right about how fast the case would be solved. Before the end of the week, two more kids were gone from our classes.

The day after the class meeting, I got to school about nine. We weren't supposed to miss school for doctors' appointments, but I'd had a braces emergency and had to see my orthodontist. I was heading down the street toward the main doors when I saw Scott Harrison, Matthew "Peeves" Rosenblatt, and their parents getting out of a big black car. Everyone was dressed up, and the somberness of the fathers' dark suits matched their grim faces. There was no disguising that something was wrong. Nobody's mother was holding anyone's hand, and for once those guys were silent. Both of them had suits on and were wearing new-looking leather shoes. No sneakers, no jeans, no loosened ties or untucked shirts. They both had this pale, polished look about them.

Next to their parents, Peeves and Harrison looked like little boys who were dressed up in someone else's clothes. I thought about turning around and walking the other way. I looked over my shoulder and glanced around, trying to find something that might give me a compelling reason to bolt back down the block. Instead, what I saw was Alexander, lumbering down the street with his shoes flopping on and off as he made his way toward me.

He was late almost every day, and today was no exception. Even though it was the middle of February, he still wasn't wearing socks, and his feet were as stinky as ever. Fortunately, it wasn't as bad when he was outside. Since December, he had been wearing an enormous black cape, which was now floating behind him as if at any moment he would soar off into the sky. He waved to me and ambled up, seemingly oblivious to who else was entering the school at that moment.

It might have been that he hadn't seen the Harrisons and the Rosenblatts, but then again, *nothing* flustered him. He'd known these families since he was five years old, and he greeted them as if there was nothing unusual about their all being at school at nine in the morning, wearing their best clothes and stony expressions.

"Hello, Mr. and Mrs. Harrison, Scott, Mr. and Mrs. Rosenblatt, Matthew, or Peeves if you prefer." He shook the fathers' hands, and one of them said, "Nice cape, Alexander."

"Why, thank you," he replied and kept right on going into school—half an hour late for his first period class, his cape still fluttering behind him. I'd slipped inside when he stopped to say hello, and he joined me on the stairs shortly. We were both heading to history class—I with an excuse for being late, and Alexander just doing what he did.

"I guess they're getting the axe right now," he said to me, running a finger across his throat.

"Yeah, guess so." I didn't know what to say.

Just then the new French and Spanish teacher came down the stairs, and Alexander called out to her, *"¡Hola, querida! ¿Como estás hoy?"*

"Alejandro, por favor, use 'usted' conmigo." She barely slowed down as she scolded him, but he just smiled and waved.

"Oh God, I adore her," he commented as she disappeared around the corner. "She's divine. But, anyway, as I was saying—the death knell's sounding just about now. Yeah ... those guys hired someone to install that keystroke recorder. Found some hacker on Craigslist and paid him a grand. Then they were all set, all set to launch their 'grand plan' and all set to use other people's accounts to do so ..." At that point, he looked over and winked at me.

"They hired someone? What are you talking about?"

"Of course they hired someone, Manny. These are people who hire out everything. They would hire someone to wipe their asses if anyone were out there offering such services. This is commonplace, standard protocol, man. Got a problem? Hire someone to fix it. This is New York City. You can hire an expert for anything, and everything can be delivered, if you know what I mean. Greatest city in the world."

I didn't really know what he meant, and by now I had stopped climbing the stairs and was just trying to take in another one of Alexander's life lessons. "Well ... where did they get a thousand dollars? And how did they get the guy into the school?"

"Hello! Where ya been? Are you living under a rock, Manny? Have you been listening to the little pearls of wisdom I give you? You gotta have dough to hire out your life, and those guys have more money than anyone—well almost anyone. Probably not more than Buns of Steel. He's got the longest hallways of anyone in the school." He gave me a knowing look when he said this and then continued. "I don't know what the logistics were of the operation, but I'm telling you, Manny, with enough money you can get *anything* done, especially in this city. And frankly, that's the way of the world, my friend. You gotta wake up and smell the cash around this place. It's ubiquitous—there's even a little bit lining these fine pockets." He made a show of pulling the lining out of one of his pants pockets. A couple of pennies, a bunch of lint, and an old piece of gum fell onto the floor. When he reached down to pick it all up, he said, "But the real question is—what's going on with the third stooge?"

"The third stooge?"

"Oh, come on, Manny. Wilkinson. George Wilkinson. Their boss. Guess they're taking the hit for him. That's what all those second bananas do. Happens all the time on *The Sopranos*. What I haven't figured out yet is what the brass did to Zimmer. They got rid of him like those nit pickers go after lice. Slam, bam—hasta la vista!" He pretended to dust his hands off as he shook his head.

By then we had reached our history classroom. I slipped in quietly, but Alexander burst in, waved hello to Mr. Hawthorne, and had his hand in the air before he'd even reached his seat. They were in the middle of a current events discussion, and Alexander had a few key points he wanted to raise about Israel. He was late, he said, because he'd missed his bus stop—he'd been too engrossed in an article about the Israeli prime minister in the *New York Times*. "How fortuitous," he declared. Mr. Hawthorne just sighed, shook his head, and asked him to get to his point.

28

Alexander was right. By Friday, our classes were down to eleven students, and there were two more empty chairs. Of course, we were eager to find out what had happened, but none of our teachers or Mitzy would tell us anything. They kept claiming that everything had to be "confidential." There were tons of rumors, and it seemed like everyone was trying to be super careful. Nobody knew what the school knew—what Zimmer had told them, or whether Harrison and Peeves had done more than turn themselves in.

Our teachers tried to carry on as if nothing had happened,

but it was impossible not to notice the differences in our classes. We almost had too much time in class without Peeves, Harrison, and Zimmer, who were always throwing everything off topic. I wondered how Simon was doing at Stuy.

Beyond the reduction in the size of the student body, there were also these dark clouds that had settled into every corner of that cramped school building, repositories of the looming fear and uncertainty about what exactly the administration knew, and whether more casualties were coming.

In the dining hall that day, while he ate three pieces of pizza and drank an enormous soda, Alexander held court. He had explanations for everything, and enthusiastically presented his theories while grease from the pizza gathered on his chin. Every so often, he would wipe it off with the corner of his cape.

"My man Manny can tell you. I predicted that those guys would get the axe. What'd I tell you, Manny? Why are people so transparent? So facile? So *jejune*?

"God," he continued, "whatever happened to good-old-fashioned school pranks, like putting a Volkswagen bug inside the building or dropping a few banana peels here and there, filling a classroom with soap bubbles? Those guys had to go and get all fancy, and now we can't use the Internet or play computer games. And how about the good old days when guys just had a beer or two, or when cheating simply involved a couple peeks at your neighbor's test? Christ, everyone's a goddamn professional these days." He shook his head mournfully before continuing. "Then, of course, there's that rat Zimmer. Don't even get me going about him. He violated the code. Big time."

There were about five of us gathered around him, hanging on to his every word while also trying not to get hit by the bits of chewed-up pizza that flew out of his mouth. Wilkinson was nowhere to be seen. He had remained intense in class and totally obnoxious about making sure our teachers knew he was working like hell on every assignment and all that, but he disappeared during free periods and lunch. Someone said he was spending all his time in the library, tucked away in one of the back carrels. Everyone suspected he had been involved in all the stuff with Zimmer, but somehow he hadn't gotten caught. And somehow nobody had done him in, at least not yet. Now I hated him more than ever.

Alexander was revved up and waved his arms as he talked. "Oh, boy, those guys went after Zimmer like dogs chasing down raw meat. Oh yeah. From the minute Zimmer put up that FaceSpace page, he was a goner, a marked man. He had so much shit on all of them; he was holding them hostage, but it was only a matter of time. What a lunatic."

"What do you mean?"

I was glad that Sam Schoenwald asked. Right now we were all starving for the details, and Sam was aggressive about going after them.

"What do I mean, Sammy? Where have you been? Been living with Manny over there out in Staten Island or something,

Sammy boy?" Alexander winked at me before continuing. "Listen here. Did you not see Zimmer's FaceSpace page? The farewell posting?"

I'd looked at Zimmer's page sometimes, but I always missed the good stuff. He was always getting in trouble with the people who ran FaceSpace, so I mostly just heard about what he did after the fact, after they'd taken it down.

"Well, it was priceless," Alexander said when Sam shook his head. "You can probably still see it if you go to archive.org. That's where the Fed archives the Web. You know, the Way Back Machine. Good stuff! You put it out there, and it ain't ever going away." He paused, took a huge sip of his soda, and burped loudly.

"Anyway, Zimmer put up this new posting that was full of pictures of him with all those guys and a bunch of girls they think are cool. Kate Brown, Elizabeth Steel, Holly Franklin. You know the Chadwick posse." At the mention of Elizabeth, I looked down. I didn't want Alexander to know anything about my feelings for her.

"They weren't real pictures, of course. Zimmer made them on the computer or something. It was that Forrest Gump thing, you know, the Zelig thing. He put himself in all these scenes with these people who despise him. People who loathe him. People who would never invite him to their parties, who wouldn't even talk to him. Probably wouldn't even help him if he were dying on the street—unless, of course, they wanted something he had. That's the kicker. Oh yeah." Alexander smirked. He knew they were all assholes, even if he didn't say it. "But that was the *coup de grace*—the death-blow—you know, the 'knell that summons thee to heaven or to hell,' to quote the Bard. Anyway, that set the 'grand plan' in motion—but it was building for a long time—had to be, with all that high-tech, keystroke recorder beeswax..."

"But did the school know about all of that—all that FaceSpace stuff with Zimmer?" I was kind of hoping that there were a bunch of reasons why Zimmer got expelled. I really didn't want the whole thing to come down to what he'd done to me. I was still kind of creeped out every day when I left the building.

"Nah. That's not how the brass did their detective work, or at least that's not the story from my sources. The brass did drag his ass in, but Zimmer knew he was a drowning rat, so he just played the part as well as he could. And of course, he got in that fabulous bitch-slapping... bam, bam! And then all that crazy-ass stuff threatening some guys' lives and all that..." He winked at me again, but kept right on talking. "That kind of thing just isn't very gentlemanly... you know. Alas, boys, I stray... now back to those emails—sent from your account, buddy." He looked over and smiled at me. "And, of course, from Buns' and Simon's, may he thrive at Stuy. Well, those emails told the story of his extracurricular activities. His *entrepreneurial endeavors*. Peeves and company ratted him out with those emails... complete with photos they'd taken on their cell phones, but because they're such morons, they did themselves in, too. What in God's name could they have been thinking? That they wouldn't get caught, despite the oh-so-clever idea to use the email accounts of the three straightest arrows in our class? That nobody would wonder who the hell was *buying* the stuff from Zimmer?" Alexander shook his head and rolled his eyes, as if he couldn't believe the stupidity of what those guys had done.

We all sat there, desperate to revel in all the sordid details, and he soon pushed on. "The brass had Zimmer cornered when they retrieved those emails, so he went in and gave everyone up—made some huge list of every St. Stephen's guy who ever got dope from him. Dropped a dime on the whole goddamn school. Then he withdrew from St. Stephen's. Yeah, he slipped the hell out of here in the dark of the night…"

Now it was clear why almost every guy in the school was walking around in perfect dress code, trying not to say shit about anything. It had been like a tomb for the past week—tons of guys must have known that they could be next, that Zimmer had ratted them out.

Alexander was shaking his head and chewing on a pizza crust when Sam piped up again. "Withdrew? What do you mean?"

"Oh, that's what the school offers you if they feel bad about kicking you out, or if they're hoping you might 'learn something from your mistakes.'" He made little air quotes when he said the thing about learning. Then he took another big bite of pizza and kept right on talking. "They ask you to withdraw. If you refuse, then you get the boot.

Some people think it's easier to get into another school if you withdraw rather than get expelled—yeah, that's a much classier act. The fizzle-out ending had to have been part of the deal they cut. Zimmer did all kinds of fucked-up stuff, but at the end of the day, Mitzy and Hutch don't want the heat around here, carting guys off to the pokey."

Alexander smiled again and slurped some soda. "The dealing aside, though, there was more. This is where it gets pretty weird. We all know Zimmer's a little…" He took his index finger and twirled it around his ear. "He had to be, given the shit he was up to, but we didn't know anything. Apparently, when the fuzz went through his computer, they found all kinds of psycho stuff. You know how he was texting all the time? Well, turns out it wasn't just your run-of-the-mill, little-white-boy drug dealer stuff. He was into all this shit with a bunch of scary freaks on the Internet. I don't know everything, but my sources say that he was into some weird shit, and his parents are sending him away, if you know what I mean. It's much bigger than your standard-fare preppy rehab, oh yeah… Harrison and Peeves are lucky he didn't whack them. Just a little bitch-slapping for Harrison and expulsion for both of them. Hell, they got off *easy*."

I didn't get everything he was saying, but I got that Zimmer was crazy. I got the creeps thinking about it, and I was pretty freaked out, too. Shit, that guy had threatened to kill me, and now I knew that he was out of his mind.

"Oh, and Manny?" Alexander looked right at me, his eyebrows raised.

"Yeah?"

"Ask your friend Henry about the Zimmer special with my best buddy Biz on FaceSpace … " He smiled at me, and I could see tomato sauce in his teeth. Then he picked up his stuff and started to sing "Taking Care of Bizness," as he left the dining room.

Everyone else left, and I sat there, stunned. What did Zimmer do to Elizabeth? And what did Alexander know about me and Elizabeth—or my obsession with her, that is. I was even starting to scare myself. The last time I'd been at the Steels' apartment, I'd snuck into her bathroom and sat there for as long as I thought I could, just smelling her flowery shampoo and going crazy, thinking about that soft, velvety skin, that long, silky hair, and those hard nipples under her tiny dress. And here I was now, sitting in the St. Stephen's dining hall, remembering me and Elizabeth out on that rooftop deck, then thinking about that crazy-ass Zimmer and what he might have done if I hadn't told my parents about his threats. I put my head down on the lunch table and took a couple of slow, deep breaths.

29

Despite all the drama that filled the hallways and the student lounge, the homework load kept coming with its Goliath proportions, and all the endless academic demands just continued in their relentless, unforgiving way. Soon we had moved beyond the tragedy of *Macbeth* and were finishing *The Great Gatsby* in English.

Shortly after the departure of our four classmates, Ms. Wright had restored her classroom. Most noticeably, she had rearranged the chairs so that there were no longer four holes where Peeves, Harrison, Simon, and Zimmer used to sit. The circle was complete with eleven students in it. All of the bulletin boards were redone, covered now with information about the Roaring Twenties and F. Scott Fitzgerald. The carpet had been cleaned, the walls had been painted, and the windows were washed. The room was one place in the school that felt fresh.

There was a new intimacy to this setting, not just because our number was smaller, but also because the major obstacles had been removed. The strange tension that had evolved between Ms. Wright and Zimmer was gone, and she no longer had to restrain herself from clobbering him when he sat in her class with a disgusted, bored look on his face, or fell asleep, head buried in his hands on the table. She no longer had to stop class every few minutes to ask Harrison or Peeves to put his chair on the floor or to take out a notebook.

Those of us who were still there, the survivors, were far from perfect. But rather than interrupting class every two minutes to settle someone down, she now had to do it only every ten. I had even discovered how comfortable it was to sit toward the back of the room and tilt my chair so that I could lean against the wall.

I tried not to do it in there because it bugged her so much, but it was easy to forget and slip into that comfy position. I had mastered the art of balancing a notebook on my thighs and taking notes in this precarious perch. Many of our other teachers didn't care whether we did this or not, and in their classes I had perfected my skills. It was one thing I seemed able to do well at St. Stephen's.

When we came to English class one day, there was a quotation from *Gatsby* on the board:

> *They were careless people, Tom and Daisy—they smashed up things and creatures and then retreated back into their money or their vast carelessness or whatever it was that kept them together, and let other people clean up the mess they had made…*
>
> *(187–188)*

I had already learned a lot of things from that novel. My classmates were expert at explaining the differences between Old Money and New Money and what the actual places were like that East Egg and West Egg were based on. I hadn't ever heard of Great Neck, but the descriptions of the houses in the novel reminded me of the Steels' place in the Hamptons. I thought about Elizabeth all the time, but I also thought about the Steel family, especially every time the novel got into all the fancy homes and parties and Daisy's voice sounding like money and all that. That was just like the Steels. It was like you could smell the money the minute you walked into their apartment. I kind of loved that. Even if it wasn't my home, I felt special just being in it, just soaking up the luxury temporarily.

Now, though, it wasn't so comfortable and luxurious for me and Henry. Ever since Alexander had told me to ask Henry about Zimmer's FaceSpace page and Elizabeth, I'd been crafting the questions I wanted to ask Henry. Yet every time I thought I was ready to ask him about it, I couldn't do it. It was like I was going around holding my breath all the time, waiting to exhale but never getting the chance. I was worried that he would find out how I felt about Elizabeth. I was unsure about my friendship with Henry, but I knew that it was the only way I stood a chance of ever seeing Elizabeth. I was willing to do almost anything to keep that possibility open.

Ms. Wright gave us a couple of minutes to copy the quotation down and to come up with three pieces of evidence for why Nick Carraway, the narrator, was right about Tom and Daisy. Also, if we thought he was wrong, fine, but we needed evidence from the novel to make our case.

Sam was done before anyone else and had his hand in the air. Alexander wasn't writing anything, but he was chewing hard and fast on the end of his pen, gearing up for something. He had some problem that made it impossible for him to take notes in class, although he often chewed on a pen or had a pencil behind his ear.

"Sam," Ms. Wright asked, "what do you think? Has Nick summarized Tom and Daisy well?"

"That's obvious, isn't it?" Sam said. "Daisy ran over Myrtle." He read from the novel: "'He ran over Myrtle like you'd run over a dog and never even stopped his car.'"

"Who is the pronoun 'he' referring to, Sam?"

"Umm ... " Sam was furiously looking back at the book. "Ummm ... I think it's ... oh, it's Tom." His face reddened.

"Well, it's Tom who's speaking in that sentence. So the 'he' can't refer to Tom, right?"

Henry raised his hand. "Look ... Tom and Daisy are

careless and able to get away with anything because of their money. Daisy kills Myrtle—Sam's actually right about that. But nobody knows she did it. The antecedent of the pronoun is Gatsby."

"Yes, that's right." Ms. Wright paused for a moment, then asked, "did you want to say anything else?"

"Yeah … Gatsby takes the fall for Daisy. And he pays with his life." Henry's voice was becoming louder. He was losing the calm way he usually spoke. "She lives with a man who has no idea what she did, or if he knows, he's going to hide it all. What was that thing Nick says about them … you know, that part right toward the end, where Daisy and Tom are sitting together, eating dinner … "

He opened his book and was flipping through it quickly, almost frantically. "Yes … here it is: 'There was an unmistakable air of natural intimacy about the picture and anybody would have said that they were conspiring together … '" He closed his book and set it on the table. Nobody in the room said anything, and after a minute or so, Henry continued. "They're both *awful*. They deserve each other." His face had turned red while he was speaking, and now he was looking down at the table while everyone in the room wondered what would happen next.

Ms. Wright waited for what seemed like an unnaturally long minute before asking, "What's the message here about money and privilege?"

George had his hand up right away. He was still slogging away, trying doggedly to catch Henry Steel and reclaim his position. He seemed more determined than ever to do so, but he never would. That was obvious, even to me. None of us, not even George Wilkinson, would ever compare with Henry academically.

"The message is that people with money have privileges, which they abuse. They can destroy other people and get away with it. They aren't held accountable for their actions." George stopped speaking and looked down at his notebook.

Everyone in the room stared at him, unable to believe what had come out of his mouth. I could see Alexander out of the corner of my eye; he was shaking his head and rolling his eyes, although for once he remained silent. It was almost as though George was daring everyone in there to indict him—but right then nobody was saying anything.

Ms. Wright looked out at all of us. Her arms were crossed in front of her, and she held a piece of chalk in her right hand. She took a deep breath and said, "That's exactly right. That's exactly what the *novel* suggests." Then she sighed.

Then for the second time that year, someone jumped up so fast that his chair crashed loudly to the floor behind him. "You are a hypocrite!" Henry pointed right at George as he spoke. He turned to leave, but right before he got to the door, George said, "So are you, *asshole*." Then he looked down at his notebook again.

I watched Henry leave the room. His stuff was still spread out on the table, and his jacket was hanging limply on the back of his chair. Ms. Wright looked at us again. George kept his head down, and I couldn't see his eyes.

"I think we need to take a break," Ms. Wright said. She went out into the hallway. When she came back about five minutes later, she handed back our essays and told us we could go.

We all kind of stumbled out of class, not quite sure what exactly had happened. I'd been planning, as usual, to ask Henry about Zimmer and Elizabeth, but now I knew I should avoid him for the rest of the day. I had never seen him become so emotional about anything. Even that day when Zimmer was screaming his head off at us, Henry had been calm. Christ, what the hell was going on? The whole school already thought that George had somehow gotten off the hook—let the second bananas take the hit, as Alexander had said. But what was the deal with Henry?

Once I was clear of my classmates, I read Ms. Wright's comments on the essay. At the bottom of the final page, there was a big B+ in blue pen, with a circle drawn around it. "Please come see me," she had written. Immediately I started to worry. This was the best grade I had gotten on an English essay all year, and now the glory was destroyed by anxiety about what had gone wrong. Something had to be wrong. Why else would she want to see me? Maybe she thought I didn't write the paper myself? I knew there were websites, like schoolsucks.com, where kids could down-load papers. Maybe she thought I'd cheated?

I became obsessed with why Ms. Wright wanted to

see me, and the minute I had a free period I went to her office. The door was closed, and I could hear her talking to another student inside. I stood in the hall waiting.

I was building my case in my mind, going over every detail of how I had written the paper. It was true that my dad and I had both read the novel and discussed it. He had also proofread my essay, circling words that he wanted me to reconsider, identifying sentences that weren't clear—but he had *not* written it.

He and my mom had made rules for how he could help me. It was too tempting for him to take over. He actually sat on his hands sometimes, so that he couldn't reach over and rewrite anything. I had been deflated by the piles of homework and my bad grades. My parents wanted to be sure they didn't add to my misery, especially when they were trying to help.

I knew that I had the drafts of my paper at home. I was thinking about how I could bring these in to Ms. Wright and show her my work when I heard her say, "George, a B isn't a bad grade. It's a fine grade." It was hard to hear the response, and I soon realized why: he was crying. George Wilkinson was sitting in Ms. Wright's office, crying over his grade on the essay. And, most shocking of all, I had gotten a better grade than he did. She had to know that I didn't cheat.

I strained to hear what they were saying, but I didn't hear anyone say anything right away. I pictured Ms. Wright handing George a tissue. I kept trying to hear what they were saying, but their voices were so low I couldn't make out anything. It was another ten minutes before the door opened, and Wilkinson walked out. His eyes were red and puffy, and his face was flushed. He was holding his essay in his hand; his backpack, half unzipped, was thrown over one shoulder. He looked at me, and I wasn't sure what to do. The hallway was too narrow for us to pass each other easily. He stood there for a moment, and I stood there, too, wondering what the hell was going on and why he wasn't getting out of there.

Then he said, "Fucking Henry Steel financed the whole goddamn keystroke thing."

"What?" What the hell was he talking about? Henry was part of the computer thing? Going after Zimmer? Sending those messages from his *own* account? From *my* account? And Simon's? I leaned against the wall, stunned. Wilkinson pushed by me and headed down the stairs.

The next thing I knew, Ms. Wright had poked her head out of the office and asked whether I was there to see her. The whole thing with my essay was lost in the back of my mind after the bomb Wilkinson had dropped. The essay crisis was blown to bits, but somehow I made my way into the office and sat down in a chair next to her desk.

Then she said, "Mauricio, I wanted to tell you how proud I am of the progress you've made. You did a good job on the *Gatsby* essay. The writing is clear and precise, and you have solid insights about a complicated novel." I stared at her as my body shifted gears. She told me to stop looking shocked and to be sure to come see her any time I wanted extra help or anything. I thanked her and stumbled out of there.

Finally, something was going well for me academically at the St. Stephen's School for Boys, but that tiny success was buried under the feelings of betrayal that overwhelmed me. It did feel like some kind of bomb had gone off—right inside my head. My brain had been blown apart, shattered to bits. I couldn't get my mind to focus on anything except the horrible feeling that someone had deliberately done the meanest thing in the world to me and couldn't have cared less.

Now I had to talk to Henry. I had to ask him about everything.

30

After a night in which I tossed and turned in bed endlessly—one minute whacking off thinking about Elizabeth and the next being outraged that her twin brother, her goddamn womb roommate, had betrayed me, had set me up to have my life threatened by Mark Zimmer—I got up and made my way back to St. Stephen's. Shit, I'd sat in that office with Mitzy and my parents, taking heat for some crime my so-called friend had committed. That asshole. I could have been expelled.

Bleary-eyed and desperate to confront Henry, I had to find out exactly what the hell he had done, although I was still totally torn. I could not imagine cutting off my link to Elizabeth, no matter how small and insignificant it was. Just the chance to walk by her bedroom door every once in a while seemed like something I could not live without. Yet I was livid and crushed and embarrassed, even. I felt foolish and humiliated... but then I started to think that there had to be some good explanation. I was desperate for one. There had to be a good reason for Henry to be involved. Whatever Zimmer had done to Elizabeth had to explain this. That was what mattered. That was what I would ask Henry about.

We were sitting in the hallway outside of our English classroom later that day. We both had a free period. Nobody else was around. I had rehearsed in my mind over and over what I would say, but now I was so nervous that I couldn't remember the script.

"Henry?" I said quietly.

"Yeah?" He didn't look up from his Latin homework.

"What did Zimmer do to Elizabeth?" I asked it quickly.

"What?" Now he looked at me. "What did you say?"

I took a deep breath. His face was red, and he was staring at me. "I'm sorry, but... I just wanted to know what Zimmer did to Elizabeth. Alexander said..."

"Alexander! Who is *he* to talk about this?" Henry was mad, but he kept his voice low. The last thing he wanted was for Ms. Wright to come out of her classroom.

"I'm sorry..."

"Don't say you're sorry! Jesus Christ. You really don't

know? C'mon! Everyone does. Didn't you check it out on FaceSpace like all the other assholes?" I had never heard Henry talk like this. All of his fancy language was gone, and the slight hint of a British accent that often colored his statements had evaporated. His face was red, and I could see a vein throbbing on the side of his head.

"No. I didn't see that … " I left out how I had frantically searched for those web pages. "But, I was worried, you know. Elizabeth … "

"Elizabeth? You don't know Elizabeth. You can't possibly know her. She would never be friends with you. She doesn't even remember your fucking name … " His voice dropped off, and he looked down at his Latin book.

It was awful to hear him talk like that, but I was so desperate to know what had happened that I was willing to do anything, even let go of what he had done to me.

"Well … what happened?" I looked at him. He was sketching something in his book. He kept drawing, and I waited for what seemed like forever. Then he looked up at me, his face still flushed.

"Okay, here's what happened. Zimmer made obscene pictures of Elizabeth. They weren't her, of course … " Now his tone was flat, as if he were talking about the weather or something.

"What do you mean?"

"He took other girls' bodies and put her head on them. Naked bodies. Bodies with their legs spread and just anything sick he could think of. Then he made pictures where it looked like he was with her—her naked. He made pornography using her pictures." He looked right at me then and kind of smirked, as if he knew that hearing this stuff made me excited. Now my face was starting to get red, and I could feel sweat on my back.

"That's fucked," I said angrily. Beneath my anger was this enormous regret at never having seen those pictures that everyone else had seen. Henry stared at me, and I started to feel even more humiliated. But I continued. "I mean, Jesus, who did Zimmer think he was?"

"Zimmer is crazy." He paused, then added, "But so is Elizabeth. Yeah, she'd never be with Zimmer. She hates his guts, although she threw herself at him every time she wanted drugs. She'd never talk to you either, especially because you don't have *anything* she wants ... "

His voice dropped off and he looked down. I had never thought about what it was like to be Elizabeth's brother. He loved his sister, but she had left him out their entire lives, and she humiliated him all the time. I'd mostly thought about how he got to see her all the time, never thinking about how he might not have wanted to see her, or that she disrupted their lives and embarrassed him and worried his family sick or anything like that.

Yet he had used my email account. I was trying to decide whether to bring this up when he said, "You know what else?" I looked at him. "I helped them. I helped them get Zimmer. I gave them money ... "

He paused for a minute, then added, "But I *never* knew

they were going to use your email account ... or mine." He looked back at his book and wrote something down.

I kept staring at him. I didn't know whether to believe him, and I had no idea what to say. I wanted to feel relief, like we were both kind of duped, like we were both these St. Stephen's losers or something. But I knew that no matter what the truth was, we had not suffered the same thing.

It felt as though someone had torn my heart out of my body and then thrown salt all over it, or thrown it down on the ground and stomped on it. Or just kicked me in the guts as hard as he could. Now I knew for sure that Henry Steel—who I had thought was my friend—was as deep in the deception as almost everybody else. And yet if somebody had asked me right then whether I would trade places with Henry Steel, whether I would give up my quiet homemade life in our two-bedroom apartment on the Upper West Side for the Steels' shiny marble world, I would have done it. That's what made me sickest of all.

We sat there in silence until the hallway filled with boys, and Ms. Wright opened the door to her classroom and invited us in.

31

We had just come out of another endless class meeting in which Hutch and Mitzy had gone over the new policies about technology in excruciating detail. There had been no mention of drug testing, and it seemed as though they were going after technology stuff first.

There were small groups of freshmen scattered in the stairwells and on the landings. I was the first one to arrive on the fourth floor, and I had just put my pack down and leaned against the wall when I heard someone shout, "Hey, Manny!" I looked around and saw Alexander sitting at the end of the hallway, kind of tucked into the corner.

He was eating a bagel with cream cheese and drinking a huge cup of coffee.

I walked over to him, and when I got closer, I could see smudges of cream cheese all around his mouth and on the newspaper that was spread out on the floor. He was about halfway through the *New York Times* crossword puzzle. Somehow he could squeeze letters into those tiny boxes, even though he couldn't take notes in class.

"Yeah?" I wished I had a napkin to give him.

"How ya doin'?"

"Ummm... okay, I guess," I couldn't figure out how he could be so cheerful when we'd just been chewed out again at another class meeting. What was also worrisome was the abuse we would soon suffer from the upperclassmen once they'd attended their class meetings and found out about the new policies. Then I realized—Alexander hadn't been at the meeting. He was always late to school and must have missed it. "Were you at the meeting?"

"Nah... I got here too late. Didn't want to barge in. I went out and got some breakfast. What was going on in there?"

I couldn't believe this guy. We had been all stuffed into that room getting told how shitty we were and how we had violated the St. Stephen's code of gentlemanly conduct and all that, and he had been out at Starbucks. "Just the usual crap about being gentlemen both in person and online and all that..."

"Oh, yeah. I know all about that. I guess the big time

spin has set in. The *other* grand plan—to distill all the trouble down to some kind of technology scandal. They could tie all the cheating into that, too, but it might be better to ignore that—or bring in some sort of circumstantial evidence beeswax. Yeah, a technology scandal will go down easier than a drug scandal … in a way … but they'll come up with something to tidy up that mess, too, sanitize it all, so the place can sparkle again. They'll find some way to sweep the illegal dirt under Hutch's fancy Oriental carpet." He pretended to hold a broom and sweep. Then he asked, "Did Hutch tell everyone not to talk to the press?"

"What? How did you know that?"

"That's what Hutch headmaster-types always do. All the papers love to whack the private school kids. They really love the girls' schools—there's nothing more newsworthy than some billionaire's daughter having a swanky party. It's particularly great if the kids get shit-faced. My favorite is when they show the parents serving the booze. Now *that's* news, but I guess the spin doctors are angling for another tale that they'll take to the *Times*. You gotta love the *Styles* section … " He laughed and shook his head before saying, "They'll go after Hutch now. He's just trying to spin some damage control. He doesn't need parents and alumni asking questions about what's going on. They're going to have to get the story right. Hmmm … something about firewalls and screening software … something about protecting the gentlemen. Christ—this crap is so transparent. When the hell is somebody going to do something original?"

Alexander winked at me before taking an enormous slurp of coffee. I stood there in amazement. He knew everything about this strange little world, and it seemed as though it was all just another day in the life of St. Stephen's to him. Hell, maybe they should have hired him to create the right spin.

I still wasn't sure about Henry, although I'd spent hours thinking about our conversation. Did he *really* not know that those guys were going to use our email accounts? That the emails were at the heart of their "grand plan"? But in some ways, I wasn't sure whether what Henry did or didn't know mattered. They might have tried to betray him, but still, now I knew that he was one of them. Maybe he was worse. He and Wilkinson. They were still here, walking around like nothing had happened, like other people were just here to clean up their goddamn messes or something.

"How do you know all this?"

"Manny, Manny, Manny! What am I going to do with you? You gotta keep up with your FaceSpace reading! It was all over there last night. There are no secrets in these places, regardless of what the suits think or what they say about confidentiality. Remember what I just said about originality— this is the same old tale, some cliché saga, 'told by a fool' and all that jazz." He looked up and smiled at me. His teeth were filled with cream cheese and small dark poppy seeds.

"I guess I was sleeping last night or something." Or doing my goddamn homework, I thought to myself.

spring

32

We came crashing into the assembly hall, three hundred boys just released from class and ready to kick back for forty minutes. We would rather have been heading out for pizza on Broadway, especially now that the weather was getting nicer, but they took attendance at assemblies so almost everyone was there. It could be a chance for a nap, especially if they were going to show a movie.

Today the lights had been dimmed, and Mitzy was standing up front at the podium. We had an assembly every Tuesday, and it was always slow going to get all of us into our seats and settled down. Today Mitzy seemed anxious to get everything going as soon as he could. He enlisted the help of several faculty members, who were circulating, telling us to find seats and stop talking.

Boys were still streaming in when Mitzy began introducing the guest speaker. Some guy named Dr. David Wilson. "Dr. Wilson works at Columbia, where his research focuses on adolescence, popular culture, and technology. I'm not going to say more, because Dr. Wilson needs to begin his presentation, which will make clear the nature of his work."

The lights dimmed, and the first slide flashed onto the enormous screen at the front of the hall. Some boys started to laugh. It was a picture of this kid with his head tilted back, drinking from what looked like a hose. On the top of the hose was a funnel. I heard Alexander behind me: "Yowza! The beer bong!"

Then another slide appeared, and there were three girls in tiny bikinis. They were smiling and waving at the camera. Someone down in the senior section made a catcall, and a bunch of kids started laughing and howling. The girl on the right had these enormous tits that were kind of hanging out of her suit. What kind of research was Dr. Wilson doing?

The next picture showed a group of guys. A couple of them were smoking cigarettes, and all of them were holding beer bottles. Some kid in the back of the hall yelled, "Let's party!" and again boys laughed and hooted. The slide changed again, and there was a collective gasp. A kid down front said, "Jesus Christ!" Then a bunch of guys started shouting stuff and cheering, and then cracking up.

On the screen was a picture of Merchant at some outdoor party. He was his usual self, so comfortable in his body, only this time he wasn't wearing a shirt and his eyes were bloodshot. He looked both exhausted and exhilarated. He had his arms around two girls wearing bikinis and sunglasses. One of them had a cigarette dangling out of her mouth. It was the cigarette that did it. The sunglasses were so huge that it was *almost* impossible to see the girl's face, but the cigarette immediately reminded me of that night back in December, out on the rooftop at the Steels' party. It was Elizabeth, up on the screen in her bikini in front of the entire St. Stephen's high school. In one hand, Merchant held a beer bottle. The other hand was squeezing one of the girl's tits. Thank God it was the other girl.

I gaped at the picture, feeling again like someone had thrust some huge dagger into my back. But now that pain was intertwined with this hungry horniness and the horror of sharing Elizabeth's bikini-clad body with the whole school. Then the next slide flashed onto the screen, and there was Colin Mason, another senior, captain of the lacrosse team. He seemed to be at the same party—something outside with lots of girls and booze. He had a two-foot-long bong in his hands, and there was smoke floating in a thin white stream out of the top of it. I wasn't sure, but it looked like it could have been the wrestling team's bong—it was kind of the same size.

The cheering had started to fade, and now everyone was sitting there in this weird anticipation, waiting to see who would get exposed next, what the next slide would reveal. Who else had seen these pictures? Even in the dark, I could make out the outlines of the faculty members who lined the walls. What were they thinking? I wondered where Ms. Wright was. She would have a thing or two to say about this, and she wouldn't hesitate for a second about doing so.

"Have you seen enough?" Dr. Wilson asked. Nobody said anything, but the image on the screen disappeared and the lights came on.

"Are these pictures familiar? Have any of you seen them before? If you haven't seen these, I've got about fifty more of boys from this school. Do you want to see them?" Nobody said anything. Nobody raised his hand. The room was silent.

"Well," Dr. Wilson said, "you don't have to say anything. You don't have to admit whether you've seen them before or not. You've seen them now. Your teachers have seen them, Mr. Mitzenmacher and Mr. Hutchinson have seen them. Your parents *will* see them. Future employers could see them." He looked around the room. "Who wants to hire someone who gets high and documents it on a public website? All of these pictures are on FaceSpace. It's a public site. Anybody can get to these pictures. Five years from now, ten years from now, twenty years from now. Some of you can't know that, given what you've posted. Now, what are you going to do about it?" He smirked when he said that, and I decided that Dr. Wilson was a nasty guy.

He waited for what seemed like forever. We had no idea what was going to happen next. We were like hostages or criminals he was trying to scare straight. I did feel relieved that I'd never created a profile on FaceSpace, but I didn't have one only because I didn't have anything to post that anyone would want to see.

"Let me read a couple of lines from a blog on FaceSpace that one of you wrote," he finally said. "'Then we were so fucking baked, hammered, shit-faced, and we went looking for girls. We found these girls from St. Mary's, who said they knew about a party we could go to. We ended up staying there all night. Free booze. The girls weren't bad; they were ready for...' I'll stop there, but if that story appeals to you, you can read more of it on FaceSpace. It gets more exciting in the next part." I couldn't help thinking that actually, yeah, I would like to know what happened next. But I was also wondering what was going to happen next in the assembly. For once, it wasn't boring.

"I'm sure that kind of extracurricular activity and the fine quality of the prose would be impressive to college admissions officers. Many check for their applicants on FaceSpace."

Dr. Wilson stopped talking again. Nobody said anything. I tried to imagine what Merchant and Mason were thinking. Their partying stories were infamous, even among freshmen. Now they were screwed.

"Why would you post pictures, on a public website, of yourself doing illegal activities? That's pretty stupid ... actually, it's asinine. And you can't get rid of this. Sure, you can take down your FaceSpace page, but the web is archived by the government. Those pages are like a tattoo: permanent. They will be with you for the rest of your lives." If the roof were ever going to blow off that building, this surely would have been the best time for that. But it didn't, and we sat there in a room where it felt like the ceiling was lowering down on us, closing in.

Dr. Wilson just kept going. "Mr. Mitzenmacher and I checked FaceSpace for each boy in the high school, and we have printed out every page we found. We will be showing them to your parents, and we will look at them and discuss them at the next faculty meeting. Don't put things in public spaces that you don't want other people to see." He paused for a few moments, and the silence felt like thick fog. Then he added, "Or maybe ... you just shouldn't do things that are illegal." Then he stopped talking. His last word was like a big boulder, hurled out into the middle of the room.

Mitzy dismissed us twenty minutes before the end of the period. Usually we would have been thrilled to have the assembly end early. Today nobody cared.

There were groups of kids scattered all over the school, talking in outraged voices to each other about how "unfair" all of this was and what assholes Mitzy and Hutch were. A bunch of boys were on their cell phones. They didn't seem to care whether they were allowed to use them or not. Mitzy's phone would be ringing soon. There was a fury in the computer labs, where everyone who could get a computer was dismantling his profile on FaceSpace as fast as he could.

Then it all clicked for me. This was exactly what they wanted. Every student at St. Stephen's was actually cleaning up the mess himself, getting rid of anything that would possibly allow *New York Magazine* or Page Six or *Gawker* to say anything about a drug problem at St. Stephen's. I had finally figured out something about how this place worked.

33

I had taken to spending my Sundays sitting in a Starbucks over on the Upper East Side. Lots of people sat around Starbucks all day long, so I figured my sitting around there for a few hours wasn't so unusual. I always brought along a bunch of books and papers, kind of buried myself in schoolwork. The only trouble was that I couldn't get anything done.

Now that my friendship with Henry had started to dissolve, I was stuck with little chance of ever seeing Elizabeth again. After strolling by Chadwick a couple of weekday afternoons, finding myself thronged by hundreds of girls, most of whom were about four feet tall and wearing plaid jumpers, I knew that it was unlikely I would bump into Elizabeth there. Or, if I did, she would be with her friends and probably wouldn't acknowledge me or anything. So I went with Plan B: sit in the Starbucks closest to her apartment and hope like hell that she would show up one day, preferably alone, although I'd take her and Kate over her and her brother.

After about three Sundays of tortured waiting, I had become familiar with the other regulars, and we'd give each other a nod upon arrival. I was right in the midst of running my eyes over a geometry proof for about the tenth time when all of a sudden, there she was. Elizabeth Steel had come in and was standing in line, waiting to order. Maybe it was because I hadn't actually expected her to show up, but I found myself unprepared—kind of shell shocked or something—and I sat in my chair, paralyzed, unable to move, think, or anything.

After the initial panic had subsided, changing into sort of a numb state of shock (more like local anesthesia than general), I kept my eyes right on that geometry proof and tried to come up with a plan. Should I walk over and say hi? Should I stay where I was and try to catch her eye? Wave her over, invite her to join me? I was sitting there kind of hunched over, staring at my textbook and trying to determine whether I was capable of walking, when I heard, "Maurrrrrrricio?"

I looked up—what choice did I have? At that point she was standing right at my table, holding some large, frothy-looking drink in one hand. In the other she was carrying a Yankees hat.

"Hey...Elizabeth..." The words kind of tumbled out clumsily, all broken up and staggered.

"Hi...how are you? What are you doing here? I thought you lived on the West Side."

"The West Side?" Somehow I seemed to forget where that was, and once again I found myself staring at her body, which from my sitting position and her standing position wasn't so hard to do, since I had to look up to see her face. My eyes just easily slid right over her tits on their way to her face.

"Yeah...you know, the West Side—right across the park."

"You're right, I do live right over there. That's right. Yes, right across the park."

She laughed when I said this, and her beautiful teeth seemed to sparkle, while that incredible heart-shaped mouth framed them so fabulously. I was once again out on that deck with her, looking right at her, knowing my life would never get better than it was that moment last winter.

"What are you doing here? Are you meeting someone?"

What? Was I meeting someone? What was she asking? Was she asking me to invite her to sit down? To join me? To sit together at that tiny table, right across from each other? Right then, right as I was preparing to ask her to sit down, to be with me, to fall in love with me and spend the rest of our lives sitting at that little table right there at the Starbucks at 87th and Lex, my arm somehow swept out toward her and knocked a bunch of my books right off the table. They crashed onto the floor, right at her feet—well, on her feet, actually.

She looked down at the books, kind of got this little smile on her incredible, heart-shaped lips, and then glanced over at the window. "Oh, hey, I've got to go..." I turned and looked, and who should be right there, out on the sidewalk, but Alexander, Henry, and Kate. Alexander was wearing a Yankees jersey and had one of those big foam Number One hands, which he was waving everywhere. Now I got why she was carrying a Yankees hat—they were going to the game.

All of a sudden, she was pulling her feet out from under my books and basically tearing out of there. "See ya," she called, as she and her shiny hair and the Yankees hat and the frothy drink sailed right out of that café.

I sat there for at least another hour, once again in a state of shocked paralysis, as I went over and over the few words we had exchanged—the missed opportunities, the stark and horrible reality that I was like some dumb little cousin to her. She hadn't thought to invite me along, even as just a friend, and despite my incredible devotion to the Mets, I would have been willing to betray them for the chance to sit with Elizabeth Steel at Yankee Stadium, cheering for anybody she asked me to cheer for. Now I hated the Yankees more than ever, and I was totally pissed at myself for blowing the one chance I'd had to let her know how much I loved her.

34

The assembly with Dr. Wilson hadn't slowed down Alexander's plans for his fifteenth birthday, although he made a point of telling me not to even think about taking pictures at the festivities, which were to take place at some bar downtown on May 1st. And we weren't going to dance around a Maypole or anything like that, despite ancient Pagan traditions of doing so, he said. It was, however, a costume party, and he promised a prize for the best costume. "And, Manny ... " he said, looking right at me, "don't even think about Superman. That's my costume."

The picture thing wasn't a problem; my cell phone was

so ancient it couldn't take a picture, and I didn't own a camera. The costume thing was a problem, though, and after hours spent trying to come up with something, I headed to the party without a costume. I'd considered coming as some other superhero, Batman or Spider-Man or something, but in the end I admitted that I couldn't pull it off. I was certain that Elizabeth would be there, and while I was eager to see her costume, I was sure that anything I wore would make me look like a fool. And I was hoping to redeem myself after that brief and clumsy encounter at Starbucks.

When I got to the party, there were tons of kids out in front of the bar, just hanging out and smoking cigarettes. Most were in costume, everything from gypsies to Vikings and princesses. I didn't recognize any of them, so I made my way through the groups gathered here and there and went in. Alexander had told me that some friend of his dad's owned the place and had agreed to "turn it over to the kiddies for a night." There wouldn't be any "official" drinks or anything like that, he said as he winked at me. Everything was going to be on the "lowdown," given all the clamor at old St. Stephen's these days.

The inside of the bar was this dreary-looking, dimly lit place that smelled of beer and stale smoke. In the middle of the ceiling was a big disco ball that was rotating kind of slowly, as if it, too, was on its last legs. It did manage to cast a few sparkles of light, which rotated across the tons of people who were packed into that place. Music was blaring, and some of the kids were dancing.

I still hadn't recognized anybody, and I was looking around sort of frantically for Alexander when I saw this guy dodging around the room, kind of jumping on guys and hugging them. I knew immediately it was Merchant. He was in this all-white jumpsuit. I had no idea what his costume was, but I was happy to see someone I knew.

A moment later I'd spotted Alexander, because Merchant ended up bouncing over to where Alexander was sitting in this booth over on the side. Alexander had on a spectacular Superman costume, complete with an enormous red cape and a huge *S* emblazoned across his chest. His hair was all slicked back, and he really looked like Superman—or at least a kind of sloppy, pudgy version of him. On one side of him sat Elizabeth, in some sort of jumper, Heidi-like dress thing, her hair in braids. On his other was Kate, fully decked out as Wonder Woman.

When Merchant got to them, he wrapped himself all over and around Elizabeth, and again I felt like I was one of the guys beaten to a pulp in the *Fight Club* movie we had watched months ago. But I made my way over to them, not sure what else to do.

"Mannnnnnnny, my man! How are you?" Alexander called out when I got over to the booth. "Hey, where's your costume, dude? Take this…" He reached into a bag on the side of the booth and pulled out one of those black plastic glasses with the big nose and mustache attached.

"Uh ... thanks," I said as I put them on. I tried not to stare at Elizabeth, who was now hard to see underneath Merchant's body. He was kind of straddling her, and she was giggling and swatting him.

"Hey, Heidi," Alexander said. "Come out from under there and say hi to Manny." She peeked out and waved at me. "Heidi's a bit busy right now with the sperm!" Alexander cracked up, and I smiled limply. Jesus, Merchant was dressed as a sperm. That was one idea I hadn't come up with, despite lots of frantic thinking about possible costumes. Then I got why he was carrying a bottle of milk, which he kept waving in Elizabeth's face, kind of spraying her with it every now and then.

"Why don't you two take it elsewhere? We got important work going on here," Alexander said to them, and Elizabeth and Merchant untangled themselves and headed off. The pain in my gut lessened slightly after they left, and Alexander gestured to me to sit down where they had just been. The bench was still warm from their bodies.

"How ya doin', Manny? Kate and I are just starting to judge the costume contest. Merchant's pretty much got it wrapped up with that sperm get-up, even if he did steal the idea from Woody Allen, but we gotta make sure all good efforts are considered."

"Yeah ... " I mumbled, hoping the glasses were covering the look of utter disappointment I was sure was all over my face.

Kate spoke up. "Hey, I'm going to check on the bartenders,

but don't leave me off the list, Alexander. I didn't stuff myself into these tight black boots for nothing, right?"

"Of course not..." Alexander pinched Kate's ass, right on her shiny little underwear-like pants, which were covered in stars. I thought she did deserve something, just for going out of her apartment in that crazy outfit.

"Alexander..." I hesitated. I was still under the illusion that he had no idea about my obsession with Elizabeth, and I didn't want to change that, but I had to know what was going on. "What's the deal with Merchant and Elizabeth?"

"Oh, Manny... it's like Life 101 with you, my friend." He patted my hand. Then he took out his silver flask, took a huge swig, and handed it to me. I took about three huge swigs and handed it back. "Manny, have you ever heard of 'friends with benefits'?"

"What?"

"You know," he said, and raised his eyebrows a couple of times. "Friends who just let you do the hoochie coochie for free—no strings attached, no need for follow-up phone calls and all that stuff. Just give you what you need when you need it..."

"Uh, yeah... sure," I said. I had no idea what he was talking about, although I wished I knew more about this thing. But then I thought about Merchant having those "benefits" with Elizabeth, and I was pissed. And what about her fucking boyfriend? "But Alexander, she has a boyfriend..."

"Not anymore... not that that ever made a difference," he said, laughing and shaking his head. "When the whole Gatsby thing went down with George and Henry, that was the beginning of the end for the Steels' ties with the Wilkinsons. The in-law infrastructure was rattled, oh yeah."

"What are you talking about?"

"Please don't tell me you missed it? The whole 'you hypocrite asshole' thing?" Alexander used this silly little voice when he repeated what Henry and George had said to each other.

"No, of course not. We all heard that."

"So..." He paused and looked at me.

"So what? What does this have to do with Elizabeth?"

"Oh, come on, Manny!"

I kind of looked down at the table at that point, hoping like hell that those crazy glasses were hiding how stupid I felt. But it was clear that Alexander knew, because he said, "Okay, man, here's the deal. The Steels *and* the Wilkinsons have piles and piles of money. Bags and bags of gold, just sitting around their castles. Enough money to buy the island of Manhattan for its value today, not the two dollars or whatever it was when the Dutch bought it from the indigenous people back in the seventeenth century. Anyway, you get my point. These people have money like you can't believe—like, even the bank has a hard time calculating numbers that big." He took another swig from his flask, handed it to me, and continued. "When you have that kind of money, there are no rules. You make the damn rules. That's why the lesser types—the millionaires, not the billionaires—get expelled. Billionaires just keep on showing up every day, just going on about their rich-ass business."

I forgot all about the room around me as Alexander kept talking. "Now, I do have to say one thing for Buns and Wilkinson," he said. "They work hard at being smart and all that. Not like that old George W. He went to all those fancy-ass schools and never did anything except some goddamn cheerleading." He shook his head at this point, and I wondered whether he would ever return to the topic of Elizabeth and what had happened between her and the other George W.

"Alas, I stray," he said as if he'd read my mind. "You wanted to know about Biz." Then he winked at me, and I was sure he was x-raying my heart, becoming completely sure I was helplessly in love *and* in lust with her. "Well, she and George never liked each other, but they shared some common interests, beyond the fact that they are both obscenely wealthy. It just kind of worked for the past few years, and of course there were all the side bars—you know, the friends with big benefits and all that. But then, when everyone found out about the connection between Henry and George, it was best for all ties to be severed. Don't expect to see Wilkinson at the Steels' swanky holiday party next year. He and his parents are for sure crossed off that guest list. End of story."

"Do you think Henry knew they were going to use his email account?"

"You know what, Manny ... " Alexander paused for a moment and looked at me as if he truly felt sorry for me. "It doesn't make any difference. You gotta get clear about these things." He took another swig from his flask, and I took another three swigs from his flask, but I felt like shit even though I was a little drunk by now. I was pretty miserable about Elizabeth and Merchant and also starting to replay the whole rooftop deck scene, trying to determine whether anything that had happened there suggested I was more than a friend with benefits. Deep down, though, I knew that there was a question as to whether I was even a friend, with or without any benefits.

That added to my misery, and although I had already started to agree that it probably didn't make any difference what Henry did or didn't know, somehow it felt worse to have Alexander confirm that—to have Alexander make it clear that Henry wasn't who I wanted him to be.

Alexander detected my misery. "Mauricio, before the night is over, I am going to find you a friend with benefits. Just let me take care of this costume contest, and then I'll find you one."

And sure enough, he did—a short girl named Jill Pennington, who was in the tenth grade at Soho Friends. She was totally cool with my putting my hands *and* my mouth all over her tiny tits, even though I didn't know what the hell I was doing. By the time we were done rolling around on the sticky floor, I was exhausted. My lips felt all kind of worn out, and my hips were sore from grinding into hers. We untangled ourselves from each other, stood up, and she said, "Nice meeting you, Mauricio." She gave me a little kiss on my lips and then she walked away, rearranging her shirt and bra as she went off.

Right then, right at that moment of extreme horniness and happy satisfaction, I was deeply in love with this friends-with-benefits thing—until I remembered that Merchant was a friend with benefits of Elizabeth's. All the way home on the subway, I dwelled deeply on how much that sucked.

35

What would Holden Caulfield have thought of Face-Space?" Ms. Wright said, and started to laugh. It was finally the last day of classes, and we had just finished reading *The Catcher in the Rye*. It was the best book I'd ever read. At last, a book I understood. And, at last, a book I loved.

Our final assignment had been what Ms. Wright called a "creative piece." We had to write about a place in New York City that was as meaningful to us as the Natural History Museum was to Holden. Ms. Wright had given me permission to write about the same museum. She said my story would be my own, not Holden's. I knew all the places that Holden had talked about. I knew the big canoe, but what I wrote about was this movie about the Amazoni Indians. I had seen it more than a hundred times.

I loved the old parts of the museum. The old parts where few people went. They hadn't been re-done, they weren't fancy. I don't think they even had air conditioning—in the summer they were hot and muggy. But those areas were like mazes, and I could wander around for hours. My mom and I had been doing that one day when we discovered the movie. It ran all the time. The minute it ended, it started up again.

I loved watching how the Amazoni Indians climbed trees. They hunted monkeys and would use blow darts to get them from hundreds of feet away. An old man even climbed these huge trees and got the monkeys. I also liked the part where these women made this huge pancake, then threw it right up on top of a thatched roof to dry.

My mom and I went there all the time. We would sit in that warm, dark space and watch. Nobody was down there. It was so quiet. It seemed as though we were hundreds of miles away from the noise of New York City—but there we were, right in the city, right inside this huge, crowded museum, hidden away, discovering how Indians lived in Brazil.

For the first time, I couldn't stop writing. All year I had struggled to write enough, always coming up short about the symbolic meaning of blood in *Macbeth* or some such thing, but this time I wrote and wrote. I kept remembering everything about the Indians and the little theater where they showed the movie and how snug and happy we always were down there. I even went to the museum again before I started working on the essay and watched the movie a couple of times. I still loved it, and I got what Holden kept saying about how these places didn't change.

I was also kind of dumbfounded when I stopped to think about those Indians in the jungle and the lives of some of my classmates in New York City. There was no way all these people were 99.9 percent genetically the same. No way.

I couldn't believe it was the last day of classes. I was thinking about that when Ms. Wright said, "Open your books to page 190. Does someone want to read?" She looked up from her book. "Mauricio," she said. Oh shit. "Mauricio, why don't you read? Start from the paragraph about a third of the way down, the one that begins with 'Something else…'"

I didn't have a choice. I had to read.

My voice kind of creaked when I started, but soon it was like I had slipped out of my chair, sort of floated away or something, and I was out there, just me and this book I loved. I was nervous, but I had the words right there in front of me, so I sort of clung to them. It was that part with all that stuff that Mr. Antolini says to Holden about what school can do for you, all that stuff about academics and education helping you find out the size of your brain and all—and using that to figure out who you are. Something like that.

I was actually kind of getting into the whole thing, despite the hint of nausea that accompanied the weird floating feeling, when Ms. Wright interrupted me and said, "You can stop there. Thanks, Mauricio." She smiled at me. Somehow she had known that I wouldn't blow up or pass out or throw up, which I'd always assumed would happen if I had to read out loud in class.

"So," she said, "what do you make of what Mr. Antolini says to Holden?"

Alexander raised his hand. "What happens right after that? What does Mr. Antolini do to Holden?"

"I was waiting for that. It always comes up. It's ambiguous, isn't it? What do you think happens, Alexander? But then let's get back to my original question."

"I don't know what happens, but it seems like Holden wakes up and Mr. Antolini is there ... " Alexander looked in his book. "Antolini is there 'petting me or patting me on the goddam head.'"

"Yes, that's what Holden says, although he 'doesn't like to talk about it.' What happens to him takes over his thoughts, just like how this discussion is being taken over by the question of what Mr. Antolini does. That's not insignificant, but it takes away, just as it does for Holden, from considering Mr. Antolini's insights. Let's not lose track of either, but let's focus first on what Antolini tells Holden about the size of his mind."

Then Henry raised his hand, and Ms. Wright looked relieved. "The scene is like so much of the novel—the mixture of profound ideas and the *seemingly* mundane ramblings of Holden's mind, the products of his acute anxiety."

I cared a whole lot less now about figuring out what Henry was saying. I wasn't desperate to be his friend anymore; in fact, we rarely talked to each other. There hadn't been any clear-cut ending to our friendship, any big blow-up or confrontation or anything, but it was like we had some ugly secret we were dancing around, trying to ignore, and it was easier to avoid each other than to sit together at lunch with all that unresolved business lurking. It was easier for me just to move on from the uncertainty of what had happened. Although I didn't stop wanting his life... his huge apartment, all that money... his sister. And I secretly hoped that I had not been crossed off the Steels' guest list.

"Yes, yes..." Ms. Wright was saying. "There is that ongoing dichotomy. It's so human, yes? One minute we're thinking about something profound and the next minute we need to use the bathroom, and that need consumes our thoughts." She stopped, then said, "But here, Holden tells us what Antolini said to him. What's significant about Mr. Antolini's points? Let's get at that."

Dichotomy? What did that mean? Henry seemed to know; he had nodded while she was talking, and now he said, "It's sort of like what happens here, at St. Stephen's. Antolini says that an academic education will help you know what your mind is able to do. Like maybe you have the brains to get an MD/PhD or become a neuroscientist. But figuring out your brain's size is complicated here because people cheat, and some people have tutors. I guess some kids find out what size minds their tutors have—that they could become writers or chemists or whatever it is that they help St. Stephen's kids get through..."

Henry was on a roll. He started talking faster. Ms. Wright was standing in front of the room. Her arm was outstretched and she was holding a piece of chalk, but she was standing still, listening to him.

"Then there are the people who do whatever they have to do to get the A. Maybe even do some of their work on their own. They grind it out day after day. They do whatever they have to do to make their minds fit whatever idea comes their way...so brilliant at producing whatever they think teachers want..." His voice trailed off, although it wasn't clear whether he was finished. Now I was pissed. Who was he to say anything about other people cheating—or being dishonest? My anger was intense, and I realized that although I kept trying to tell myself that I'd moved forward, I hadn't. Perhaps I never would.

Alexander looked over at Henry, rolled his eyes, and shook his head. Then he raised his hand. "Holden needs Xanax."

A bunch of boys laughed, but Ms. Wright said, "That's not such a funny idea. It's revealing about what's happened with medication. There are a lot of options now that weren't available at the time when Holden was worrying compulsively. Something like Xanax might have helped him. Last year a student thought Ritalin was what Holden needed. But drug therapy aside, focus on the book. Does Mr. Antolini offer Holden anything?"

I started to raise my hand, but then put it down. Ms. Wright looked around. She had seen me, and now waited to see whether my hand was down for good. My mind was racing, as I tried to plan a comment. What could I say about Holden and not give myself away? Was there anything I could say that would not make me look like a fool in front of my classmates, in front of Henry? I had read this part about five times at home. I kept thinking about what size mind I had. What size was the C+ mind?

"Mauricio?" Jesus Christ. She did it again. Today was going to be a record-breaker. I had already read out loud, and now I was going to say something. It was now or never. It was the last day of class. I would have to wait until the fall if I wanted to say anything again. I was terrified, but I wanted to say something—I wanted to take on Henry Steel.

"Ummm...I think Mr. Antolini says something important..." She waited, not interrupting me, giving me time to muster up more courage and keep going. I saw that a couple of guys had their hands up. Ms. Wright asked them to put them down. "Ummm...that seems like it would be great, you know, like knowing the size of your mind might actually be, uh, like a way to be honest about who you are...umm, although throughout the book Holden seems to be so aware of everything—to know so much about all the *phonies* and all that. That drives him crazy. The phonies really make him crazy..."

I stopped talking and felt my body sink into my chair. I

was relieved to be done talking, but then I started to dissect what I had said. How many times did I say "you know" and "umm"? Did I tell these guys too much? Were they all thinking that my mind had to be about a C+? Did Henry know that I was talking about him? That I thought he was one of the phonies? He had to. He knew everything. I didn't look up, kind of just sat there.

"I agree, Mauricio. There's something critical here about being honest with ourselves about who we are and who we might become." She smiled and then called on the guys who had their hands up before. The discussion carried on all around me, but I could have been anywhere. It was like being in the midst of some busy, crowded place where you don't know anybody; you are alone, despite having people surrounding you.

I just couldn't participate anymore that day. I'd had two big moments during class—that was more than I'd had all year. Finally, I'd had something to say and I'd said it—although the question of being honest about who I was still dogged me. A lot of what had happened to me that year had been about discovering that I longed to be someone else, someone with money and power and sexy women. I was forever concocting fabulous fantasies, full of wild images of myself as this big powerful man, this tycoon . . . this St. Stephen's gentleman.

36

"Why would anybody waste words writing about Wilkinson—even in this thin tissue of yellow journalism?" Alexander was looking at our school paper. "This is *news?*"

I was surprised that Alexander would be surprised. The school newspaper was basically just a bunch of upbeat stories about St. Stephen's. Whatever was going on beyond the front doors of our school wasn't in our paper—the editors left that to the *New York Times*. Instead, they focused on school "issues" and repeatedly got worked up about the dress code or the food in the cafeteria or some other big, important topic. Still, their versions of the stories always had a spunky, cheerful tone to them.

The story about Wilkinson was even more positive and enthusiastic than the usual pieces, and Alexander speculated that his parents had commissioned it. Or maybe Wilkinson had written it himself and paid some dope on the newspaper staff to act as if it were his.

"Listen to this," Alexander said, and read from the article in a stuffy British accent. "Although he is the third generation of Wilkinsons to attend the St. Stephen's School for Boys, George Wilkinson has decided to leave after his freshman year. He will attend St. Olaf's School in Littleton, New Hampshire, where he believes 'the sports will be better.' Oh, this next part is great!" Alexander switched to a whiney, nasal tone. "'I've always wanted to go to boarding school. I like dorm life. I had that at camp.' Man, I gotta talk to the editors about this crap. I get the need for whitewash, but this saccharine bullshit goes too far. Hell, maybe I'll start writing for the paper. It sure would have been a great time writing about Harrison and Peeves taking the hit for Wilkinson and Steel." Alexander threw the newspaper into the trash can in the mailroom. We had gone in there to get our essays and exams. I had pulled mine out of my mailbox and quickly stuffed them into my empty backpack.

"It's time to line up," Mitzy poked his head into the mailroom and called to us. Everyone in the high school participated in the graduation procession, and we were getting ready to line up on the sidewalk in front of the school. The ceremony was going to take place at Lincoln Center, where there was a theater large enough to hold a couple thousand people.

When we were standing in line, arranged from tallest to shortest, I was kind of right in the middle. I was feeling happy that at least I wasn't a little shrimp of a guy, and also that I wasn't near Henry, who was at the front with Wilkinson right behind him. While we were standing there, I could see Ms. Wright making her way down the line, stopping every couple of boys and asking them to straighten their ties. "When *you're* a senior, I will make sure that all the freshmen have their ties correctly knotted in your honor. Today is not a day to make a unique fashion statement." When she saw me, she stopped and said, "Mauricio, good job on the final assignment. I made a copy. May I use your creative piece next year with the freshmen?"

I was stunned. She wanted to show the freshmen something I'd written? And not because it was terrible, exactly what they shouldn't do? "Uh … sure," I mumbled.

Ms. Wright smiled at me. "Have a great summer, Mauricio." She continued down the line, telling boys to straighten their ties or tie their shoes or fix up anything that wasn't just how it should be. Fortunately Alexander had on loafers (without socks), or there might have been a battle. Just when she got to the end of the line, we started to move.

Right before we entered the theater, I saw them. Elizabeth

and Kate were standing to the right of the doors. They appeared to have again coordinated their outfits, their hair, and even the sunglasses perched on their heads. Kate still looked like a second-rate version of Elizabeth, like the fun-house mirror image or something. They were waving and calling out to boys. Of course, I started to worry about whether they would call out to me.

When Wilkinson passed them, they both turned away—Elizabeth more dramatically than Kate. She pulled her sunglasses over her eyes before turning her whole body away from the line. He pretended not to see her.

I was thinking about how amazing she looked when I heard my special name. "Maurrrrrricio! Hi!" Elizabeth and Kate were waving and smiling at me. I held up my hand and gave them a little wave. "Hi."

"See you in the Hamptons!" Elizabeth called out right as I entered the theater. Alexander had invited me out to his family's place. He said it wasn't any kind of estate, but it would give us a place to flop. Hell, I didn't care. I would have stayed at a bus stop if it meant I would be anywhere near Elizabeth.

Kate and Elizabeth had talked their parents into letting them spend the whole summer out there. They were planning to get jobs. Alexander laughed when he told me about their "ambitious plans." I couldn't have cared less about what they were doing; I just wanted to be a part of Alexander's "Bizness." Apparently Henry was heading off to a high school program at Oxford, to study criminal justice or some such thing. Alexander had laughed his head off when he told me about this. I was relieved that I wouldn't have to fear running into him. He could study whatever he wanted, just as long as he was an ocean away.

We headed down the center aisle of the theater. The rows of seats were full, and everyone was standing and clapping. Cameras flashed, and there must have been hundreds of video cameras rolling—every other face had a camera in front of it. We weren't even the seniors; they would file in after the underclassmen.

When I sat down, I looked up at the ceiling. It seemed miles away from me. Hanging from it were glass chandeliers, each one with hundreds of little gleaming drops of glass hanging down, the light appearing to reflect off every tiny crystal.

As I looked up at that ceiling, I realized that finally there was enough space—in this enormous room—to allow three hundred blue-blazered high school boys to breathe. We weren't packed in on top of each other today. We weren't crowded. We didn't have to push and shove to create space for ourselves. We didn't have to brush up against the person sitting next to us and fight with him over who got the armrest. Now that there was finally enough oxygen, nobody cared about getting the armrest. There was finally enough air for all of us. We could breathe at last.

Up on the stage, at the podium, was the valedictorian— the boy with the highest grades in the senior class at the St. Stephen's School for Boys. He looked like an ordinary guy.

You'd never have known that he had the highest grades. His speech was even a little boring.

I was kind of listening to him, while also thinking about the Hamptons and Elizabeth, when he said, "We're brothers at St. Stephen's. We come to love each other as deeply and as ferociously as brothers do." Ferocious love? Deep love? I liked Alexander a lot, but most of the time he was off doing his own thing, spouting off about this and that, and I was his dumb little sidekick, his eager audience, his desperate protégé. Originally, I'd thought I liked Henry. Then everything imploded. I was still trying to figure out whether I had ever really liked him or just wanted to be near his sister, hanging out in his enormous apartment, eating Mrs. Carrothers' homemade cookies and hoping for an Elizabeth sighting, or maybe just the chance to walk by her room.

I had no idea on that final day of freshman year what would go on to happen, and I sat there on that last day kind of listening and also wondering what Henry would say when he stood at the podium in three years. It was inevitable that he would have the grades to be valedictorian and so would give us some words of wisdom at our graduation, no matter how full of shit he was or wasn't.

One by one, each senior's name was called, and the boy went up on stage and got his diploma. Some of them put their arms up in the air proudly; others just took the diploma, shook hands with Mitzy and Hutch, and made their way quietly back to their seats. Regardless of what they did, they all looked the same, covered in big black graduation robes. It took a long time for all seventy-five of them to get their diplomas.

There was a reception outside on this big patio right after the ceremony. Excited parents ran around snapping pictures of their sons, gathering groups of boys together and insisting on documenting the day. Seniors wrapped their arms around each other and posed. Their gowns were unzipped, and their mortarboard hats were scattered all over the ground.

A bunch of them were smoking cigars, and they looked like bankers celebrating an enormous deal they'd just closed. They looked as if they all liked each other. All of them hanging out, smoking cigars, hugging each other, and posing for their parents' cameras.

I couldn't imagine hugging my classmates the way these seniors were hugging each other. I couldn't imagine posing for picture after picture, our arms draped around each other, our smiles enormous. Guys I had never seen together looked like they were best friends. They were all in this thing together. They were all happy—at least that's what it looked like.

I took one last glance at the scene and started to walk away. I didn't know most of these guys. This party was for them, not me. I was just a puny freshman—or sophomore now, I guessed.

Right as I was walking away, I felt this huge weight clamp down on my back and these enormous arms wrap around me, making it impossible to move. "Maaaaaaaaaaaaaa aaaaaannnnnnnnnnnnny!" Merchant had me in an enormous bear hug and was lifting me off the ground, practically shaking me up and down.

"Hey," I managed to squeak out, from inside his body-crushing hug. With his body wrapped so tightly around me, I could smell traces of cigar smoke, beer, and some kind of deodorant soap. He put me back on the ground and when I turned around to face him, he held out his right hand and proceeded to crush my hand as he shook it. "Hey, man, keep going with the wrestling. Go for it! You know … " He kind of slowed down for a second, then looked me right in the eyes and said, "We all sucked at first." Then he smiled at me, pumped my arm up and down a few more times, and shouted, "Long live the Tribal Brotherhood of the Barbaric Yawp!" Before I could respond, he ran off, yawping loudly as he jumped on some other guy's back and began thumping him.

About ten seconds later, when I was almost half a block away, I heard, "Hey, Manny!" And there was Alexander sprawled out on the steps of some synagogue. He was smoking a cigar, and he had taken his shoes off.

"Hey, Alexander."

"Manny, my dogs are killing me," he said, pointing at his red-looking feet and puffing away on the cigar.

"Yeah … looks that way." His feet did look awful. All raw and pink. I didn't say anything about how wearing socks might make his leather shoes more comfortable.

"You know, Manny, you're okay. There's that problem with the Mets, but you will learn, my man Manny. Live and learn … and, about Buns … well, let's just say that when you got that kind of cash, you gotta do what you gotta do." He took a big puff on his cigar, then added, And you know, with a brain that big … " He paused and puffed away some more, then said, "It's gotta be hard to get your head off the pillow in the morning. Think about it." He was leaning back on his elbows, more comfortable and relaxed than anybody else would ever be on some hard cement stairs in front of a synagogue on Broadway, just watching people walk by as he reclined there, smoking a cigar. "I'll call you soon about the Hamptons."

"Thanks, Alexander. That'd be great."

I walked up Broadway a couple of blocks, then stopped when I was sure Alexander couldn't see me anymore. I sat down on a wooden bench in front of a deli and pulled the essays and exams out of my backpack. My hands were shaking as I flipped to the back of each one, searching for the grade. B- after B- after B- stared at me. The one higher grade was a B+ on the English piece. But despite this small bright spot, I began to feel that I would die and on my gravestone they would carve "Mauricio B- Londoño." Mr. B-. It wasn't a good grade, but it wasn't *that* bad. I guess I was even a little relieved they weren't C's or even C-'s. My grades could have been worse.

I didn't know what I was hoping for. All year I had gotten low grades—not much was going to change right at the end. And these grades were better than anything I had gotten even two months ago. Somehow, though, I had harbored this false hope, sort of like what leads people to buy lottery tickets. But I hadn't won the lottery. I was still one of the few middle-class kids at St. Stephen's, and I had gotten a bunch of B-'s. My grades were as middle class as I was.

I stuffed everything back into my backpack, stood up, and continued to walk up Broadway. My backpack was lighter than it had been all year—all that was inside were those essays and exams. It was so light I could barely feel it on my back. It felt unnatural. It felt weird, like I had lost just about everything.

What would I do with myself tonight? I had no homework. I had nothing I had to do. It wasn't like I wanted homework, but I couldn't believe the year was over. Five boys who'd started the year with us wouldn't be back next year. I felt like some kind of survivor, yet having gotten to the end of the first endurance test, I wasn't *really* sure what to feel. Maybe I had done more than simply survive?

37

I was pretty hungry by then. I looked around and right down the street was my beloved Gray's Papaya. Just the thing and cheap. I loved the bold signs declaring that they were "friendly New Yorkers." Ms. Wright had used that as an example of an oxymoron early on in the school year.

I went inside and ordered two hot dogs and a large papaya drink. I paid, got my food, covered the dogs in mustard and sauerkraut, and stood at the counter. I felt kind of happy, kind of jovial even.

On one side of me was this tiny old lady, who had a metal shopping cart that was almost bigger than she was.

She also had two dogs and a papaya drink. Her cart was filled with clothes and shoes and soda cans. It was warm outside, but she was wearing layers of clothes and even had a scarf wrapped around her neck. She had an absurd amount of makeup on, and her lips were outlined in a way that looked like she had used a black marker to do it.

On the other side of me were two guys about my age, wearing baggy pants and sports jerseys. They also had the requisite Air Jordan sneakers. I felt odd, sandwiched between these people. There I was in my khaki pants, button-down shirt, school tie, and blue blazer. I was even wearing new leather shoes that were now killing my feet, although at least I was wearing socks.

Soon I had dripped mustard on my tie. The way my feet felt started to spread throughout my body, as though at any moment my outfit might strangle or suffocate me. And yet I liked how I looked. I'd felt good that morning when I looked at myself in the mirror—I looked important and handsome. I looked like I had money. I'd kept looking at myself, imagining Elizabeth right there, her arms wrapped around my neck and kind of peeking out from behind me, looking at us together in the mirror and smiling, rubbing her body right up against mine. I liked that image. Loved it, actually. I also liked the way the seniors had looked at graduation, in their best suits, smoking cigars. They were so proud and confident, so certain about themselves.

There was so much talk about how St. Stephen's was the best school, but then there were some kids who were assholes, who were dishonest, who would do whatever they had to do to get ahead. It all kind of seemed like a fat lie. But still, every day I walked in those big heavy front doors, I was proud I went there. In fact, I was *thrilled* I went there. And then there was Alexander. I had never in my life known anyone like him. Somehow Alexander made it feel like it was no big deal to sell your soul for money, even though he saw straight through the bullshit, too.

I liked how people in the city reacted when they asked where I went to school, and I responded "St. Stephen's." They got excited and treated me like I was special and super smart. I liked that, even if they didn't know the truth about some things. I liked the credit I got, even if I didn't deserve any of it.

I must have stood at that lunch counter for an hour, watching people through the window. The old lady and the kids were long gone by the time I left. My feet hurt more than ever, but I'd loosened my tie and taken off my jacket. I balled it up and stuffed it in my backpack, then kept walking even though my feet felt as though little knives were stabbing them all over the place.

Elizabeth had looked beautiful, standing there when we marched by. Her honey-colored hair was long and shiny and silky, and her lips were all shiny, too. What if she became my girlfriend? The idea was crazy. Henry *and* Alexander had pretty much made that clear, and deep down I knew it myself. But maybe she liked me? I started thinking about kissing her. I started picturing us out on that deck again. I would just lean over, casually, so casually, so cool and calm and suave and all that, and kiss her right on her shiny, heart-shaped lips.

Right then and there I promised myself that I would kiss Elizabeth Steel. I wouldn't leave the Hamptons that summer until I had done it. It seemed like such a small thing, especially when compared with what my classmates said they did with girls, and with my late night fantasies about her. Maybe it was a small thing. Maybe it was a tiny little puny thing, no big deal. One kiss. But it felt huge. To get close enough to kiss her, I would be able to smell her, to touch her. I kept picturing her when she'd waved to me before graduation. She and Kate were wearing these flowery dresses. Really short. Happy dresses.

I kept walking and walking, thinking about Elizabeth and the school year. For some reason, I started thinking about Mark Zimmer and wondered what he was doing now. Even Alexander, who knew everything, didn't have any information about Zimmer. We knew he wasn't ever coming back to St. Stephen's.

Then I started thinking about Henry Steel and George Wilkinson. They were both from families who seemingly had everything, at least according to Alexander, who always seemed to know the length of everyone's hallways. The longer the hallways, the bigger the bank accounts. Yet both of those guys seemed kind of miserable.

Some day, I promised myself, I would have long hallways. Just as I would kiss Elizabeth that summer, someday my hallways would be so long that even Alexander would be impressed. But *I* would be happy. No, make that *jovial*. I would cruise up and down those hallways in the most jovial fashion imaginable.

That's what I hoped for on that final day of freshman year, but here I was now, three years later. I still hadn't kissed Elizabeth, but I was finally a graduate of the St. Stephen's School for Boys. I sat on that hard wooden bench, staring at the plaque with my special name on it: Mauricio Londono. Maybe losing the tilde was a small price to pay for all that I still hoped the school would do for me.

About the Author

After many years in New York City, Susan Fine said goodbye to Zabar's and Gray's Papaya in search of an affordable apartment. She, her husband, their two young boys, and 10,000 pieces of Lego landed in Chicago, where they love everything except the weather. When she isn't reading *The Dangerous Book for Boys*, she's working on her second novel. A former English teacher, Susan can still hear a me/I error from about a mile away. For assistance with sorting out the me/I conundrum, check out pages 110–113 in her first book, *Zen in the Art of the SAT*. For more equally interesting tidbits, visit Susan online at http://susanefine.com.